MW01531685

remembering REDBANK

A COMING OF AGE NOVEL BY

JACK COLEMAN

This book is a work of fiction. Names, characters, places, and incidents are the product of the author's imagination or are used fictitiously. Any resemblance to actual events, locals, or persons, living or dead, is coincidental.

Copyright © 2012 John W. Coleman
All Rights Reserved

ISBN-10: 1478227192
ISBN-13: 9781478227199

LCCN: 2012912780
CreateSpace
North Charleston, SC

To Jean

*my beloved wife, without whose tireless efforts and patience
this book would never have been completed.*

TABLE OF CONTENTS

IT ALL BEGAN LIKE THIS...

High school is a wonderful part of a person's life, or at least it certainly should be. I know that I learned far more in those four years than was written in all the books I studied. Little did I realize that so much adventure could be crammed into such a short span of time. Most of what I carried away from high school had much more to do with life experience than formal education. Please allow me to explain

The year of 1947 had been a great year in Redbank, Shawnee County, Virginia. The local high school in our county of only 2,437 people (according to the 1940 census) had won the state basketball championship and the football team had gone undefeated. This was a great accomplishment for our small town of less than 1,500 people, counting men, women and children. The town was on a high seldom reached.

But that had been last year. Now things seemed to be changing. Five starters from the championship basketball team had graduated, along with the quarterback, two running backs and all seven linemen from the football team. What kind of season could we possibly have in either football or basketball? Would we even win a game, much less excel in either of the sports? I suppose I could quote what Charles

1

Dickens wrote in "The Tale of Two Cities," *It was the best of times, it was the worst of times.*

Redbank was the county seat and that alone put us in a class by ourselves. The other high school in the county classified us as their archenemy. We dared not wear our school colors when we were in their town, nor did they wear their colors when they came to Redbank. That was how things had always been and they were not about to change.

Our high school class of '52 numbered exactly 52 members in the fall of 1948. There were thirty boys and twenty-two girls. Every one of us expected to graduate, however time certainly proved us wrong. Only forty-one survived to the final day when the diplomas were handed out. The other eleven? A couple of the guys dropped out and joined the army and three or four just stopped coming to school after their sixteenth birthday. It was rumored that two of the girls got in a family way and in those days you just didn't come to school having swallowed the so-called watermelon seed. An out-of-wedlock pregnancy was frowned upon and considered to be a disgrace.

Five of the members of our class had started first grade together. There was me, Jack White, along with my two best buddies Jack Algood and Fred Smith. Also in this select little group were two girls, Anne Adams and Betty Mason.

The five of us were always together. Jack Algood and I were special friends and were sometimes even referred to as the two Jacks. We almost shared the same birthday, but Jack Algood had been born four days before me. Any time you saw one of our group, all you had to do was look around and the other four would be close at hand.

We all came from what was referred to back then as good families. My mom and dad had been born on farms outside of Redbank and after they married had moved into town buying a small house on Jackson Street. It's interesting to note that every street in our town was named after a confederate general.

Mom was a housewife and my dad had a small but prosperous insurance business that provided a comfortable living for our family. Dad was a deacon in the Presbyterian church and my mother served as president of the Women's Fellowship.

Jack Algood's father was a foreman for the electric company, having worked his way up from grunt to lineman and then to his present position. He had been with them for twenty years and expected to retire from the same company. Jack's mother took care of their house and occasionally baked for others in town. Her specialties were pies and cakes.

The local dairy company was run by Fred Smith's father and his mother was a housewife looking after their four children. There was always a big supply of ice cream in their fridge and Mrs. Smith would offer a heaping dish of it to everyone who visited. I liked to stop by Fred's house after school because I knew what was waiting for me there.

Now let me introduce you to the girls, Anne and Betty.

Anne's father was a doctor, a gynecologist. Apparently he was very successful because the Adams had one of the largest and finest houses in town. Dr. Adams had come from the Tidewater area before going to The Medical College of Virginia in Richmond and then on to John Hopkins University in Baltimore. While completing his residency, he met and married Anne's mother who had been a nurse. Anne told me that her dad had also practiced medicine at the prestigious John Hopkins Hospital in Baltimore where she had been born. The family had moved to Redbank when Anne was two.

Dr. Andrew A. Adams was very flamboyant and known to be somewhat of an eccentric. You could recognize him a mile off by the way he dressed. In the summer Dr. Adams always wore a white linen suit, red tie and matching red socks. Perched on his head would be a white sailor straw fedora with a feather stuck in the wide red hatband. This outfit was completed with black and white wing-tipped shoes. In the winter months, Dr. Adam's white suit would be exchanged for a grey wool double-breasted suit and the familiar sailor straw for a white rancher's Stetson with the trademark red band and feather. You could say that Dr. Adams was a real dude!

The doctor's car was also one of the largest and fanciest in all of Redbank. It was always the latest model black Cadillac four-door sedan with white sidewalls. According to what I had heard, Dr. Adams was a poker player of note and the envy of all his poker buddies. He played at least once a week in a high-stakes game at the Antler Club.

Our little group of friends was rounded off with Betty Mason. Her family lived near the Adams but in a somewhat smaller home. Betty's father was on the county school board, having previously been the principal of Redbank High School. He had some sort of higher degree in education from the University of Pennsylvania. Her mother had been a teacher but now stayed at home and took care of the house and Betty, who was an only child. I liked Mrs. Mason who was a very nice lady. Mr. Mason, I guess I should really call him Dr. Mason like everyone else did, was straight-laced and expected Betty's friends to have the very best of manners.

And so the five of us looked with great anticipation toward the fall of 1948 wondering what the new school year would bring.

CHAPTER 1

SUMMER 1948

The summer of 1948 before school started seemed to drag by. The five of us did some fishing and a lot of swimming in the creek. But you could only drop your line or jump off the big rock so often. To put it bluntly, we were bored. It was probably because all of us guys were anxiously looking forward to going out for the football team, the Red Raiders. Many of the starters from last year's undefeated team had graduated so it looked as though all three of us might have a good chance of making the team. We were all considered to be large for our ages and that was a big plus.

The girls were also making plans for the football season. They both intended to try out for the cheerleading squad and were very confident that they would do well and be selected. Being a cheerleader for the Red Raider team was every girl's dream.

Football tryouts were scheduled for the first week of August and we could hardly wait. Every evening for the past three weeks we had joined several guys from town at the high school field, running laps and tossing a football around. We wanted to be in the best possible shape for the first day of tryouts. We had even stopped drinking sodas and eating candy because we had been told that the coach didn't allow sweets and junk food to pass the lips of any of his players. No smokers or tobacco chewers were even allowed to try out for the team. Tobacco was a total no-no for Red Raider teams.

The night before the tryouts were to be held, the five of us met behind the church under the big pine trees. This had been our private meeting place since we were all in grade school. The pastor may have thought that we gathered there to pray, but we were really just exchanging updates on what had been going on in our lives over the past few days.

"I heard that there are some guys coming in from Central who weigh over two hundred pounds," Jack Algood remarked.

"If that's true then at least fifty pounds must be pure fat. Those farm boys eat like food is going out of style," I replied.

"Yeah, that may be true, but they can also build some pretty big muscles lifting all those hay bales," Jack said seriously.

I was not about to be intimidated. "Muscles are not all it takes to make the team. You have to be smart and fast and crafty. You need to be able to react quickly. We'll beat them out in no time. It's not going to be a problem."

"Don't be so sure of yourselves," Betty Mason added. "You go out there on the field all full of yourself and you're going to fall down flat. Or more likely, you'll be knocked down flat. Mark my words."

"Oh, Betty, don't be such a pessimist," Anne responded. "Look at the bright side of things. Our guys here have hard heads and that's really all you need to play football."

I had heard enough from the girls. "A lot you know about it," I told Betty and Anne. "You don't even know how to throw a ball overhand. And those guys from Central aren't so special. The three of us will make the team without any problem. You'll see," I assured them.

Our conversation under the pines continued on for over an hour with most of the talk centered on the unknown factor of those who would be at the tryouts from the other districts.

Finally Fred said, "I'm thirsty! Let's go over to the Sweet Shop and get a soda or something." So much for our resolution to give up sodas.

Redbank was in a farming region and there were four secondary schools that fed into the high school. The farm kids went to the nearest school for their first eight years and then came by bus to the high school for their final years of schooling. We had met some of them before at church and vacation Bible school, but for the most part they would be total strangers. Little did we realize that among these newcomers there would be three or four who would soon become our close friends. You can never really know what the future holds.

The summer before my freshman year, Dad finally allowed me to take a real job. Up to that time, the only thing he would permit me to do was to have a paper route. There certainly wasn't much money in that. I had fifty customers and I only received two cents per house per day. All that work for only seven dollars a week. And to make matters worse, Dad required that I put five dollars into a savings account from which I was only allowed to withdraw fifteen dollars at Christmas. I never seemed to have any money.

But I heard that a new hardware store was opening that was owned by a man who had just moved to Redbank. And on one day in June as I was passing the store, I noticed that the owner, Mr. James, was unloading merchandise from his truck. It was hard work and he looked really tired. "Would you like some help with that?" I asked him.

He looked me over and responded with a smile. "Sure, kid. I can always use a helping hand."

I ended up working with him that day for about two hours. After we had finished, he thanked me and offered me a cold bottle of Coke. As we sat down together on the curb, he asked me, "Do you have a part-time job?"

"No, sir. Not really. Just my paper route."

"You seem to be a good and willing worker," Mr. James replied. "I need someone like that. Besides, I have never had anyone volunteer to help like you just did. I like your can-do spirit."

"Are you offering me a job?" I asked.

"I sure am! I need someone after school and on Saturdays to fill in where needed. You seem to be just the kind of boy I need. I'll start you off at seventy cents an hour. How does that sound?"

I was elated. "Wow! It sounds great to me, but I'll have to ask my dad if it's okay with him. I'll go over to his office and ask him right now."

Dad said I could take the job with the condition that it didn't interfere with my schoolwork. I quickly ran back to tell Mr. James that my dad had given his permission and to ask when he wanted me to start.

"How about tomorrow?" he responded.

I had a real job making real money. I began the next day and worked eight hours a day until football practice started. I was making thirty-six dollars a week less tax. The first week I was able to put twenty-five dollars in the bank and still have five dollars in my pocket. There was no more need to sneak in the back door of the movie theater since I could now afford to pay the fifteen-cent ticket price. I could even spend ten cents for popcorn.

It wasn't long before I learned that my new boss had a fourteen-year-old daughter named Barbara. I met her my first week on the job and it was love at first sight. Barb, as everyone called her, was a really nice girl. She informed me right off that she didn't like to be called Bobbie or Babs, but preferred to be known as only as Barb or Barbara. She was about five foot seven inches tall with long blonde hair. Her hair looked almost white when the sun was shining on it. Barb had bright blue eyes and the cutest smile I had ever seen. She seemed to really have what it takes and I was attracted to this new girl right away.

A couple of days later, I pumped up my courage and asked Mr. James if it would be all right to take Barb to the movies on Saturday night. He looked at me with surprise and said, "You are the first young man I have ever met who would ask permission to take my daughter to the movies. I like that. Sure, you certainly can, that is if Barb wants to go with you."

I couldn't wait to get to a phone to call her. "Hi, it's Jack. Would you like to go to the picture show with me on Saturday night? I hear that there's a really good movie showing."

She hesitated before replying. "Well, I guess so, Jack, but I'll have to ask my mom if it's all right with her. Hold on for just a minute."

The minute that I waited seemed like an hour. But the good news was that her mom had no objection. Somehow I knew that this was the beginning of something really great.

Saturday night finally came. I went by Barb's home and spoke with her mom who told me what time to have Barb home that evening. As we left the house, I thought, "Her mom is a really nice lady. I bet that Barb will grow up to be just like her."

Before we even got to the theater, Barb and I were good friends. She was so easy to talk to and we had a great time just walking along together. We found out that we liked many of the same things. We both enjoyed the same kind of music and sports and were both even interested in church. In fact, she told me that her family was going to transfer their membership to the church we attended.

That evening I introduced her to several of my friends who were also at the theater. In a small town like Redbank going to the movies was about the only thing to do on a Saturday night in the summer. Everyone, young and old, went to the movies.

After the show ended, we stopped by the Sweet Shop, the local ice cream parlor where the teenagers hung out, because I wanted her to meet all of my friends that were there.

On the way back to her house, I got up my courage and reached for her hand. Happily she took mine. I made sure to get her home ten minutes before the appointed time. My mother had always told me that first impressions count a lot and I certainly wanted to make a good showing with Mr. and Mrs. James.

It wasn't long before I was spending lots time with Barb on the phone and even more with her in person. We started taking walks or riding our bikes together after I finished work. One evening as I was on my way over to Barb's house, I ran into Jack Algood and he tagged along with me. In fact, he even ended up joining Barb and me as we took our nightly walk around town.

As we neared Main Street, we met Anne Adams. When I introduced Barb to Anne, I was surprised to find out that they had already met. That evening the four of us formed a fast friendship that would last throughout our high school years.

CHAPTER 2

FOOTBALL AND BARB

That first evening when we were all together, Anne asked Barb if she was going to try out to be a cheerleader. Barb sadly shook her head. "I don't think I would have a chance of being selected since I'm a newcomer to the school," she replied.

And it was true that usually only the well-established and most popular girls at Redbank High were chosen to be on the squad. But Anne was quick to assure Barb that it probably wouldn't be a problem for her at all. After all, Barb was a lot cuter and more athletic than most of the returning cheerleaders. "You'll make it, Barb. I'm sure of it," Anne encouraged her. "We can be on the squad together."

That sounded like good news to me. Jack and I were going to make the football team and Anne and Barb would be there cheering us on. This meant that we would be seeing a lot of each other since the cheerleading squad went to all the away games and even rode on the same bus with us. Maybe the coach would even let us sit together. Of course it all depended on Anne and Barb becoming cheerleaders and Jack and I making the team.

The tryouts for the football team went great. Coach had us fall out in shorts and tee shirts and started us off by running ten laps.

Following that, we were led through a number of strenuous exercises. By the time we had finished them, everyone was soaked through and exhausted. We had just begun to catch our breath when the coach had us on our feet again to line up and run wind sprints. This involved running twenty yards at full tilt, counting to twenty and then running twenty yards more. Five times we repeated the drill. Finally the coach had mercy and gave us a couple of minutes break before making us repeat the whole process on the return down the field.

Not once on that first day did we even see a football, much less touch one. "If this is football," I thought, "I'm not at all sure that it's for me."

But that thought never entered my mind again, even though the next day we once again repeated the laps and exercises. All of us were totally exhausted when the coach finally sat us down on the bleachers and gave us a real pep talk and laid out his training schedule.

Finally we were allowed back on the field where we were divided up by weight and height. The bigger guys would be linemen and the smaller would go in as backs. I had envisioned making touchdowns, but instead I was put down as a lineman. It looked like I was going to be used as a blocking dummy or some such thing.

Little did I realize that the ends, the pass catchers, were also considered as linemen. When the footballs were finally brought out, the coach took all of the linemen aside and had us go out for passes. I caught every ball that he threw my way and before I knew it, I was an end. The rest of those chosen were to be the guards, tackles and centers.

Here I was a freshman, but chosen to be running with the first squad. In fact, I started at right end in the first game and played that position in every other game. I was in my glory. That freshman year I caught two passes for touchdowns. In my mind I was on my way to being selected for the All State team. I was even beginning to think that I might be awarded a four-year scholarship to the University of Virginia. Freshmen who make the starting team can have some really big dreams and I was dreaming big.

We won our first three games, tied the fourth and then lost the fifth by just one point. We closed the season out by winning our last five games for a record of 8-1-1. This was not a bad record for a team that had lost ten starters from the year before. I had played in every quarter at right end and gotten some recognition by catching those two touchdown passes.

Jack Algood had also made the first team starting at halfback. During that year he had scored six touchdowns, made several long runs and was a big star. All the girls were really impressed by Jack and kept trying their best to impress him and win his attention.

But Jack only had eyes for Anne. The two of them were considered to be "an item" at school. And Barb and I had also started going steady. It was great to really belong to someone and be known as a couple. At the school dances, no one ever bothered to cut-in on the two of us. I'm sure that some of our classmates envisioned us as getting married someday. In fact, those thoughts had even danced across my mind on more than one occasion.

I attended my classes and kept up with my studies, but my life really revolved around two things--football and Barb. In my sophomore year, I once again played right end in every quarter and scored three touchdowns. Jack Algood continued to be the star halfback, gaining a lot of yardage on the ground and racking up ten scores. The team went eight and two for the season and in the final game we lost by just one point. We only had three loses against sixteen wins in those two years. It was certainly not a bad start for our football careers. We were on our way to seeing all our dreams become a reality.

CHAPTER 3

LIZZY

Fifteen is a great age to grow up in a small rural Virginia town. I continued to work at Mr. James' hardware store after school and on Saturdays. And I also continued to see Barb every chance that I got.

It was that summer between our freshman and sophomore years that some of us guys bought an old car. Jack Algood, Fred Smith and I included Jim Scott, a new kid in town, in on the purchase. The car was a 1928 Model A Ford sedan, a Standard Roadster. It didn't run and had been in the back of a barn for several years where it must have served as a chickens' roost. The car was a mess, but we didn't care. We had a whole year to fix it up (and clean it up) before even one of us would be old enough to get our driver's license, much less be allowed to drive it on the highway.

We paid the grand sum of fifty dollars for this wonderful chariot and spent every spare moment we had working on some aspect of getting that old car ready for the road. I didn't know a thing about engines, but Jack Algood and Fred Smith had fathers who were pretty good mechanics and they were always willing to help us when we hit a problem. Of course, our big problem was money. But isn't that always the way with most first cars?

By Christmas of that year the engine was running, but the big drawback to getting the car on the road was the purchase of tires. They cost a lot. According to the Sear's Roebuck catalog, a tire with tube to fit our car would cost twenty-five dollars. But we didn't need just four tires, we also needed a spare. The fathers who were helping us with the repairs insisted that we have a good spare. What it boiled down to was that we were going to have to pay one hundred and twenty-five dollars plus shipping for the tires and tubes. That was a fortune. I figured it would be summer before we would be able to come up with that kind of money. But it was actually the second week in May when the tires finally arrived.

What a great day that was when we were able to take the car out for a short drive around the block. We decided that we needed a name for the car and unanimously decided to call her Lizzy. Each of us took a turn at the wheel but didn't dare go out of the neighborhood since there were no tags on the car. Hopefully none of the neighbors were looking out of their windows to see our illegal vehicle puffing down the side street.

On May 31st, Lizzy became official The license plates were put in place and we could at last proudly drive down Main Street beeping the horn at everyone. Jack and I had both received our drivers' licenses the day before on my birthday. The guys decided that as a birthday present they would allow me to be the first driver. Can you imagine driving your own car right after your sixteenth birthday? What a tremendous thrill it was!

Our Model A took a lot of our time that summer. When we bought it, the car was a dingy dark green with black fenders. Since green was one of the colors of a rival school, it just didn't seem right to drive a car with their colors. So we decided to paint the car bright fire engine red and white, the school colors of Redbank High. It may not have been the greatest paint job, but the car certainly stood out in a crowd. We painted the body red and the fenders white. In order to make our automobile even more special, we painted her name, Lizzy, in big white letters on both of the front doors. Everyone wanted to ride in Lizzy, particularly after we had just won a game. On such occasions we would pack in as many people as we possibly could into the old car and cruise Main Street blowing the horn. OOGA-OOGA! You could always hear us coming. Lizzy was the big sensation of the school year. In fact, a picture of our car graced the first page of the 1950 school yearbook.

We did have a couple of problems that had to be faced with Lizzy. Where would we park her each night and how were we going to manage paying for the gas and oil she would need? The gas and oil part was easy. We decided that we would each put in five dollars a week to cover the cost. We quickly learned that it took lots of money to be car owners.

There still remained the question of where we would park Lizzy at night. Jack and Jim each had space for her in the small barns behind their houses. Nearly all of the older homes in Redbank still had small barns where the buggy horse and perhaps a cow or two were sheltered in the olden days. But the new homes like mine, which was only thirty years old, had garages with only space for one car.

After much discussion, it was decided we would keep Lizzy at a different house each night according to a roster that we drew up. Lizzy would just have to spend half of her nights outdoors. But surely, we figured, that had to be much better than staying in that old barn with the chickens where she had been kept for so many years.

Gas turned out not to be too much of a problem since it was selling for less than twenty-five cents a gallon. But even that amount cut pretty deeply into our money supply each week.

Then Fred came up with a brilliant idea of how to lower the gas expense. He had heard from a college friend that you could save money by taking gasoline, kerosene and water and then adding a bit of laundry soap to the compound. What did we have to lose? It was worth a try.

So we would take a gallon each of gasoline, kerosene and water and then mix that combination together with a handful of Ivory Flakes in a five-gallon bucket. As amazing as it seems, the car would actually run on such a mixture. She smoked a bit more than usual and would backfire on occasion, but seemed none the worse when she was filled with this witch's brew. Perhaps Lizzy was somewhat harder to start, but we found we could overcome that if we primed the fuel pump with pure gas before we tried to crank her up. All we had to do was squirt some gas from a small oil can directly into the fuel pump and she was ready to carry us all off on another day of adventure. And our fuel costs were lowered by about a third.

No one could miss seeing our red and white Lizzy as she rattled down the street trailed by a billow of grey smoke, an occasional loud bang caused by her backfire and the continual blowing of her horn with its distinct OOGA-OOGA sound. We were the proud owners of the most spectacular car in the whole district.

CHAPTER 4

THE PURCHASE

The car had taken a lot of my spare time between my sophomore and junior years in high school, but it didn't distract me too much from my love life. Barb and I were still going strong and Jack Algood and Anne had a real tight bond as well.

But something would occur that would change all of that. That summer before our junior year I made what turned out to probably be the biggest mistake of my young life. I bought an old pistol.

I guess a lot of boys dream of owning some kind of gun. My dream gun was a pistol rather than the rifle that most of the guys wanted for squirrel and rabbit hunting. I guess I got the idea from watching too many cowboy movies.

Growing up I had all sorts of cap pistols, but none that would actually shoot any kind of projectile. Many of my friends had received the popular Red Ryder BB guns, but my mother was afraid that I would shoot someone's eye out so I never got one. Anyway, I wanted a real bullet-shooting pistol. But the fulfillment of childhood dreams can sometime lead to big trouble. Mine certainly did.

It all started one Saturday afternoon in June while I was working at the hardware store. An old fellow in bib overalls came into the store carrying a small bundle wrapped in burlap. He asked me if the owner was available and I went to call Mr. James.

I listened in as they talked. The man said that his name was Norman Smithers and that he lived up on the mountain just west of town. Times had been pretty tough, he said, and he needed some cash. He had brought in a pistol that that he owned hoping that he could sell it to Mr. James.

My boss informed him that he didn't buy or sell pistols, but only shotguns and rifles. Although ammunition for pistols was sold in the store, he didn't have a license to deal in handguns.

The old man looked really disappointed. "I need some cash to pay for some medicine for my sick wife," he explained. "Can't you make an exception this one time?"

But Mr. James stood firm and told him that there was no way he could help him out and that he didn't know of any place in town that would buy the pistol from him.

"Well, thanks for your time," the man said as he left the store.

I hesitated for a minute or two and then slipped out the back door to find the man with the pistol. He was only about a block away from the store standing on the corner looking very downcast.

"I heard you talking to my boss about a gun you wanted to sell," I whispered to him. "Would you consider selling it to me?"

"Only if you have cash money," he replied. "I have to have cash."

"How much do you want for the gun?"

Mr. Smithers hesitated a moment and then asked, "Could you manage twenty dollars?"

"Sure. I just got paid. But we can't make a deal like this here on the corner." Suddenly I felt exposed standing there on the street negotiating to buy a gun. "Can you meet me in the alley in back of the hardware store in a few minutes?"

"I'll be there," the old man said with a smile.

A short time later I managed to slip out of the back door of the shop to complete the deal. I realized I didn't even know what kind of a gun I was buying. I learned that the pistol was a .38-caliber revolver with a five-inch barrel. Mr. Smithers warned me that it had one cracked chamber on the cylinder.

"It shouldn't be any problem though," he informed me. "Just be sure you don't put a shell in that chamber and you'll be all right."

I was anxious to complete the sale. "You said you want twenty dollars? Is that right?"

"Yep," he replied. "Twenty will do it if that ain't too much."

I continued my questioning. "Do you have any bullets for the gun?"

"Nope, but your boss said he sells them right there in the store."

"All right. It sounds like we have a deal." I took the money out of my pocket. "Here's the twenty dollars."

"And here's your new pistol," he said handing me the gun. "Be careful with her and she will last you a long time. And thanks. I really need the money."

I quickly took my new treasure into the store and hid it temporarily behind some merchandise near the corner of the storage room. Since I had picked up some things for my mother at the grocery store earlier, it was easy to slip the pistol into the bag and take it home with me.

There were two major problems that I immediately faced. Number one: Where was I going to hide the gun? And number two: How was I going to buy ammunition for it?

I had a solution for the hiding place all worked out before I even got home. In the garage, on a shelf behind dad's snow tires with some other junk, was an old Hopalong Cassidy lunch box. I used to carry it to school when I was in the fifth grade. I had scratched my name on the back of the box because so many of the other boys had lunch boxes just like mine. No one had touched the box for years. The pistol would certainly be safe there.

The problem with the cartridges took care of itself on Monday afternoon. Mr. James had gone to the freight office to pick up some packages and I was alone in the store. This gave me the chance to get a box of ammunition, put the money for it in the cash drawer and to make an entry in the book where we kept careful track of all ammunition purchases. I wrote down that someone named Jed Martin had bought a box of twenty-five shells for a .38 revolver. That night I hid the bullets in the lunch box with the pistol.

But where and when could I fire my precious pistol? I thought of that old limestone quarry just north of town. It would be the perfect place to try out the gun. And Saturday after work, just before dark, would be the perfect time. Everything was falling into place.

On Saturday I took the pistol along with the box of ammo to the store with me in a paper bag and once again hid them in the storage room. After work, I just picked up the bag and carried it out to my bike that I had ridden to the shop that morning. It was just a short ride out to the quarry, but it seemed to take forever.

On my arrival, I made sure that no one was around and then slipped down into the quarry. I quickly set up a target that I had made and hoped I could hit it. Carefully I loaded the pistol, stepped off about twenty-five feet and took aim. I had waited a whole week for this moment and I was excited. Slowly I squeezed the trigger. There was a tremendous explosion. Sparks flew everywhere as black smoke rolled out of the gun, which I had dropped on the ground. Wow! What a kick! A moment later I realized that my hand had been burned.

What had gone wrong? Was the ammo too powerful for the old gun? Did it have two cracked chambers? I didn't know what the problem was, but I did know one thing. I would never fire that pistol again. It was way too dangerous.

So I took the gun home with me and hid it once again in the Hopalong Cassidy lunch box on the shelf behind my dad's winter tires. Sometime later I told Jack Algood about the pistol and where I had stashed it. Best friends don't have secrets from one another. Besides, I knew I could trust Jack. He would never tell anyone.

CHAPTER 5

THE DIABOLICAL PLOT

A really terrible thing happened later that same month. Not to me, but to my best friend, Jack Algood.

It happened one night in late August of 1950 when Jack and Anne were saying goodnight on her front porch. They were kissing and Jack had his hand under her blouse when Anne's father, Dr. Adams, stepped out of the darkness. He had just parked his car in their barn out back and was walking onto the porch when he spotted the two of them. It was not that they were kissing that infuriated him, but the fact that Jack's hand was up under the front of Anne's blouse.

"What do you think you are doing to my daughter, young man?" he yelled, grabbing Jack by the shoulder and pulling him away from Anne.

"Uh, uh...I was just telling her goodnight, sir," Jack stammered.

"Whatever gave you the idea that you could take advantage of Anne like that?" her father continued, his face turning red with anger.

"What...what do you mean?" Jack asked, trying to sound innocent.

"You know exactly what I mean!" Dr. Adams shouted. "Anne, how long have you allowed this boy to do such things to you?"

By this time Mrs. Adams had come out having heard all the racket. "What in the world is going on out here. What's all this noise about?" she asked.

"This young fellow was sexually assaulting our daughter and I caught him in the act," Dr. Adams informed her.

"He was doing what?" Mrs. Adams screamed.

"He had his hand under Anne's blouse. And look! Her bra is even undone!" Turning to Jack, he shouted, "Get off my property this moment and you keep your hands off of my daughter! In fact, let this be the last time you ever speak to her. DO YOU HEAR ME?" Dr. Adams was bellowing at the top of his lungs.

Jack quickly backed away, turned and ran for his life. He had never seen a grown man so angry. I truly believe that if Dr. Adams had a gun in his hand, he would have taken a shot at Jack.

I had just left Barb's house and was walking toward home when I heard Jack running for all he was worth down the street behind me. As he approached I could see even in the dark that Jack was as white as a sheet. He looked like he was nearly scared to death.

"What happened to you, Jack?" I asked him. "Did someone jump you or something?"

As Jack caught his breath, he related the whole incident to me, adding that he and Anne had been petting pretty regularly the past month or so. Jack even claimed that she had started it. I could hardly believe that. Anne was a nice girl and nice girls just didn't do things like that. At least none that I knew about.

Jack had really messed up his love life and there was little he could do to fix it. He had been forbidden to ever see Anne again and it didn't sound like Dr. Adams was going to change his mind about that anytime soon. But at least Barb and I were having no problems. Everything was still going great with the two of us.

The news of what had happened that night at Anne's house didn't take long to reach Barb. Anne had called her just as soon as she could get to a phone alone and had told her the full story. What Barb learned, and that Jack and I didn't yet know, was that Anne had been grounded for a month. The worst part was that her folks were planning to send her off to a private girls' school miles away as soon as they could arrange it.

Talk about shattered lives. A bomb had gone off in our midst. And to make it worse, it had a terrible effect on all of our lives. It seemed like our foursome had been reduced to just two people. Would things ever return to normal again? Only time would tell.

A month went by. School started and we had our first football game of the season. Anne was still in town. I would see her in school and also in church on Sunday morning sitting between her father and mother. When the last amen was said, the three of them would be the first ones out of the church door. They would go directly to their car without even waiting to shake the pastor's hand.

At school Anne was seen only in the company of other girls and she had dropped out of the cheerleaders. Rumor had it that she would be going to Staunton to attend an all girls' school in the very near future. But as it turned out, the school had no vacancies and so it would be at least January before she could be enrolled. Anne was still going to school with us, at least temporarily.

Her mother would drop her off just before the starting bell every morning and her father would be there to pick her up when school let out. Anne didn't attend any of the football games that fall even though we were having a great season. We won eight games in a row, tied the ninth and won the last.

One Saturday night in early October, Barb and I were sitting in a booth in the back of the Sweet Shop when Jack came in and joined us. He had been down in the dumps ever since the incident when Anne's dad had caught them together. Jack was having a terrible time with his schoolwork, as well as on the football field. He just wasn't the same old Jack.

We asked him to sit down with us and tried to cheer him up a little. I even bought him a scoop of chocolate ice cream, his favorite kind, but nothing seemed to work. It was as though he couldn't concentrate on anything. I think he was in mourning over his loss of Anne.

Suddenly Barb's face lit up. "I have a great idea," she informed us. "This is something that can solve Anne's problem and yours too, Jack Algood. This is how it will work." Barb then proceeded to outline an elaborate plan full of intrigue and deceit. I would have never thought she was capable of coming up with such a devious plan.

"This is what we will do," she began, turning to me. "First, you and I will stage a breakup. If both you and Jack Algood agree, we could even do it right here tonight in the Sweet Shop and get things started. The more people who are aware that we are no longer going together the better."

Barb leaned close to me, her voice not much louder than a whisper. "After everyone knows that our relationship is over, then I can begin to date Jack Algood. But you understand that I won't really be dating him. It will all be just a pretense. Jack will just act like he is taking me to the movies or a dance, but he will really still be seeing Anne. And I'll still be seeing you."

Barb's plan wasn't making much sense to me. I tried to catch the gist of what she was saying but it just wasn't computing. Was she saying she was going to pretend to date Jack Algood? What about me?

Then Barb gave me my instructions. "Here's your part, Jack White. You are going to go to Anne's house and ask to talk with Dr. Adams. I'm sure he'll see you. And then you're going to ask her father's permission to take Anne to the movies on Saturday night. It will be easy."

I guess I should have seen the red lights flashing, but I just nodded my head and let Barb continue unraveling the plan.

"You will have to be very polite, Jack," she advised me. "You will need to always address Dr. Adams as sir and always call Mrs. Adams ma'am. They will eat it up. They won't be able to resist you. Don't you remember how my dad loved it when you asked his permission to date me. This will work I guarantee it."

"But, Barb," I argued, "I don't want to breakup with you. You're my girl and I like you a lot. We get along just great and we don't ever quarrel. I don't feel good about this plan you've come up with at all."

Barb wasn't about to take no for an answer. "You're jumping to conclusions, Jack White. We won't really be breaking up, only making it possible for Jack and Anne to be together again."

She smiled sweetly at me and took my hand. "Don't you understand? Whenever you pick up Anne to take her out, Jack Algood and I will be waiting to meet you somewhere. Then all we have to do is switch dates."

Barb sounded so confident that I almost started believing that her plan might possibly work. "Don't worry," she reassured me. "No one will ever know because no one will ever see us together. We'll keep it all under wraps. Only the four of us will know what's going on. It's simple really."

I ran the plan over in my mind and concluded that it might actually be possible to pull this off. "Yeah," I said quietly, "it just might work."

Those were the words that Barb had been waiting to hear. Before I even knew what was happening, she was on her feet shouting at the top of her voice and moving away from the table. "Jack White, you keep away from me!" Barb yelled. "I never want to see you again! I hate you and we are finished! Just stay away from me! It's over!"

What an actress Barb turned out to be. Everyone in the shop stopped talking and eating and gave their full attention to the scene that was taking place. Barb put on quite a show! I had never seen anything like it. Giving me a final dirty look, she turned on her heel and rushed out of the store.

The plan was under way whether I was ready for it or not.

Two evenings later, I nervously phoned the Adams' home. After identifying myself to Mrs. Adams, I asked if I could come by and speak with Dr. Adams for a few minutes. I strained to hear Mrs. Adams talking to her husband in the other room as I waited on the phone. And then came the answer. "If you are here by six-thirty, the doctor will be able to see you."

Barb's plan worked like an absolute charm. Dr. Adams was completely fooled by my politeness and even invited me into their fancy parlor so he could get to know me better. After asking a few very direct questions, Dr. Adams gave his consent for me to see his daughter. I had to promise him that I would have Anne home at a decent hour and that I would never allow her anywhere near Jack Algood. Dr. Adams made no secret about his feelings toward her former boyfriend.

As he shook my hand at the door as I was leaving, I assured him that all I wanted was to see Anne back to her former happy self. "I know I can trust you," Dr. Adams said. "You're a good boy."

And so plan was put into operation. I would go by once or twice a week and pick up Anne at her house. Her parents would be there to see us off and I always remembered to use my very best manners. The two of us would leave for the evening with their blessing. As soon as we had rounded the corner, we would immediately head for a preselected spot where Barb and Jack Algood would meet us. All we had to do then was switch girls. Usually the four of us would do something together in a nearby town, but every now and then Jack and Anne would slip off by themselves for some private time. Barb and I were still as much in love as ever, so we enjoyed being alone with each other too. Everything was perfect. Maybe too perfect.

At the end of these special evenings, we would meet at an appointed time and place. Jack would kiss Anne goodnight and then I would take Anne home, careful to get her back to her house in time to meet her curfew. I trusted my friend, Jack, to take Barb safely back to her door. It was amazing how well everything went. There really were no problems. Barb was truly a genius when she hatched this plan.

No doubt about it, teenagers can really come up with some devious plans. Some, but not all, work to perfection. This seemed to be one of those perfect plans that couldn't possibly fail.

CHAPTER 6

A RUDE AWAKENING

Everything did go great for several weeks. Then on November 12th, the storm broke. It was a Monday when Anne told Barb that she had missed her period. When Barb relayed the news to me, I didn't exactly understand what she meant. I was a teenage boy and teenage boys just don't really know much about some of those girl things.

"What do you mean missed her period?" I asked feeling really stupid.

"Anne thinks that she might be pregnant," Barb replied.

I shook my head. "That can't be. She's not even married."

Barb looked at me in amazement. "I can hardly believe that some guys are so uninformed about the facts of life. At least you are, Jack White," Barb admonished me.

She then proceeded to tell me that Anne and Jack had been having some really torrid petting sessions and that finally one thing had led to another. She assured me that it was very possible that Anne was pregnant.

It was almost too much for me to take in. "What are they going to do?" I asked, wondering if there really was any answer to a problem of this magnitude.

"Anne wants to run away to Maryland and get married," Barb said.

"Married! They're too young to get married. Besides, Jack doesn't even have a job. How will he ever support a wife, much less a wife and a baby?"

Barb gave a long sigh. "Those details haven't been worked out yet, but Jack says he will come up with something."

"What a mess!" was all that I could reply.

Two nights later Anne's parents found out about the expected baby and things really got bad. Since I was the one who had been seeing Anne, they of course thought that I was the guilty party. But Anne finally broke down and told them that the only person the father could possibly be was Jack Algood. She admitted that she had been dating Jack on the sly. Her dad threw a tantrum when he heard that news. Not only was Anne pregnant, but she had been living a lie and deceiving them.

According to what Anne later told Barb, her father had forced her into his car and driven her and her mother over to his office where he had given Anne a shot that caused her to pass out. And right there in the office with his wife who had been a nurse assisting, Dr. Adams performed an abortion on his very own daughter.

I couldn't believe my ears. It was like some sort of nightmare.

Apparently after he had completed the abortion, Dr. Adams took Mrs. Adams and Anne home, where he ordered his wife to pack suitcases for the three of them. The family then drove to Hot Springs where they checked into a suite at The Homestead, a world-famous resort hotel. During the seven days they were there, Anne was not allowed out of their suite. And when they returned home, Anne was locked in her room and forbidden to see or talk with anyone. The school was notified that Anne had a virus and was very ill.

All of this came to our knowledge when Anne finally was able to make a phone call and tell Barb what had transpired over the past two weeks. You can imagine that Barb immediately called me and then I phoned Jack to pass the news on to him.

When Jack learned what had happened, he went into a rage. Using language that I had never heard from him before, he shouted, "I'll fix old man Adams' boat! He'll never be able to harm Anne again! I'll fix him!" And having said that, he slammed down the phone and I was left wondering what he meant.

Early on Tuesday morning, I began to find out.

It was about seven-thirty when the doorbell rang. I was still asleep since school didn't start until nine. Several rings of the doorbell were soon followed by loud knocking which woke me from my sleep.

I heard Dad talking to someone downstairs. Their voices were muffled, but I could hear my father say, "Jack's still upstairs sound asleep."

Then an unfamiliar voice loudly stated, "We have a warrant for his arrest. Get him downstairs this minute." There was a slight pause and then, "No, never mind. You wait here. We'll go up and get him ourselves."

I sat up in bed. Arrest? Whose arrest? Who was downstairs anyway? What was happening? I was still half-asleep, trying to make sense out of what I was hearing.

Suddenly my bedroom door burst open and a Virginia state trooper rushed in followed by Redbank's chief of police, Bernie Dotson.

The state policeman looked straight at me and demanded, "Are you John C. White, better known as Jack White?"

I nodded my head and answered, "Yes, sir. I'm Jack White."

The policeman then issued an order. "I want you to get up immediately and get dressed, young man. You are under arrest for the murder of Dr. Andrew A. Adams."

"What do you mean?" my dad interrupted. "Are you trying to tell me that you're arresting my son for the murder of Dr. Adams? Andy Adams is dead?" My father paused to catch his breath. "This can't be happening. It's impossible. My son would never do anything like that."

The policeman tried to calm things down. "I'm very sorry, sir, but a warrant has been issued for your son's arrest. We are going to have to search your house and garage for evidence right now."

Turning to me, they told me to get out of bed and get dressed in clean clothes. The clothes that I had worn the previous night were put into a bag marked "Evidence" and quickly removed from the room.

I was handcuffed and then marched down the stairs and out to a state police cruiser. I was placed in the back seat and the door was closed and locked. My head was spinning. It was too much for me. Everything was happening so quickly and nothing was making sense.

My mom and dad hurried out to the car just in time to speak a few encouraging words to me before the trooper drove me away.

"Don't worry, son," Dad shouted through the closed window. "There has to be some logical explanation for all of this. I'll get a lawyer and see you at the jail in a little while."

My mother just stood there on the sidewalk and cried. Her baby was being taken away in handcuffs by the police. All our neighbors were standing nearby watching the heartbreaking scene. It was like a bad movie.

When we arrived at the jail, I was taken to a small windowless room. The handcuff on my right wrist was unlocked and then reattached to a metal ring bolted to the table where I was ordered to sit. Without saying another word, the two policemen then walked away

There were dozens of bewildering thoughts racing around in my brain. I couldn't make any sense out of anything that was happening. I was overwhelmed by all the questions that had no answers and problems that had no solutions. It was like I was having a bad dream and I couldn't wake up.

I sat there in the silent room for what seemed like an eternity. I was absolutely alone. There was no one to supply any answers or clue me in on what was happening. Finally the door opened and the state trooper walked in followed by a man in civilian clothes.

The policeman was the first to speak. "This is Mr. Aaron Johnson, the state's attorney. He has some questions for you and I would suggest you answer them fully and honestly." No one advised me of my rights. In 1950 in rural Virginia, the arrested party was considered guilty until proven innocent.

Mr. Johnson took a seat at the table opposite me, laid a folder of papers on the table and took out a long yellow pad and his pen. The policeman stood by the door like he was keeping guard.

I was the first to speak. "What's going on? Why have I been arrested? I haven't done anything wrong."

Mr. Johnson held up his hand to silence me and stated, "I'll ask all the questions here, boy! Are you John C. White? Do you live on Jackson Street in the town of Redbank, Virginia?"

My voice was shaky as I replied, "Yes, sir. But please tell me what's going on. I don't understand what's happening."

"Just a minute and we'll get to all of that. But first, a couple more questions." He paused for a second or two before continuing, "How old are you and what is the date of your birth?"

That was an easy question. I relaxed a little and replied, "I turned sixteen on my last birthday. I was born on May 30th, 1934 right here in Redbank."

Mr. Johnson seemed to ponder my answer. "So, you are still a minor then. That might be a problem," he murmured. "You just keep on answering my questions real honest like and things will go a lot better for you."

Right there and then I decided to tell the truth about everything that he asked me. Suddenly I recalled a Bible verse, *"You shall know the truth and the truth shall make you free."* The verse came to me right out of the blue. I knew it was from the Bible, but I didn't recall anyone ever saying that to me. Maybe I had heard it in church. Obviously I had never read it because I never read the Bible. But now this scripture verse was etched across my mind.

Mr. Johnson continued to question me, but it was somehow different. I had a peace in my heart. It was like I used to feel as a kid when

I would hurt myself and come crying to mom for comfort. She would take me on her lap, smooth my hair, kiss me and say, "That's all right, son. Everything is going to be fine now." When that happened, suddenly everything would change and I would feel much better.

Hearing those words from the Bible in my mind had brought me the same kind of comfort and had given me confidence that even though I seemed to be at the bottom of a deep pit, it was going to work out just fine.

The questioning continued for over an hour and not once did I vary from the truth. I even told Mr. Johnson that the night before I had parked with Barb James up on Breezy Summit and that we had necked for nearly an hour before I took her home. It was pretty embarrassing telling an adult that I had been kissing a girl on a dark hilltop while I was parked in my dad's car. But that was the truth and I was not going to sway from it. The attorney had taken notes on everything that I told him, occasionally asking me to repeat something that I had said previously.

Finally Mr. Johnson took an official looking paper from his briefcase, looked at me very sternly and read: "John C. White, you are being charged as an adult with the premeditated murder of Dr. Andrew A. Adams. You will be formally charged in open court within twenty-four hours at which time you may be represented by council."

He then instructed me to sign at the bottom of the paper from which he had just read. With that, he turned on his heel and marched out of the door followed by the policeman.

I felt numb. I had answered all of his questions, but no one had answered any of mine. I had not even been allowed to ask my questions. It was the darkest moment of my young life.

In a few minutes the policeman returned. He unlocked the handcuff from the table and took me through a door that opened into a long hall. As the metal door clanged shut behind us and we started walking toward my cell, all I could think was, "Oh, God. Please help me!"

I was put into a single cell, the handcuffs were removed and the door locked. Again, I was alone, left to ponder the events of the last couple of hours. Thoughts continued to pour through my mind like a rushing river. I was afraid and it seemed as though I had every reason to be frightened.

There was no place to sit except on the filthy bunk that was chained to the wall. The bunk had no sheet, blanket or pillow, but only a dirty, thin blue and white striped mattress. In the corner was a toilet with no seat or toilet paper. Over on the other wall was a washbasin with only a cold-water tap and with no soap or towel. I was to learn later in the evening that the water was only turned on in the morning and again in the evening. And even then it was only turned on for ten minutes each time.

Over all, I would have rated the jail as totally horrible. The building was well over a hundred years old having been built sometime before the Civil War and added onto many years later. I might have been in the same cell where Yankee prisoners had been held. It certainly looked that old. In my cell was a barred window without glass. If I wanted to, I could jump up and grab the bars to pull myself up to see outside. When I finally did, I found that I was looking at the back wall of the Court House. Certainly not much of a view. I was obviously not staying in a first class hotel.

About two hours passed before the jailer, an old fellow with a badge pinned to his grimy police shirt, came in to tell me that I had visitors. He stood me up, cuffed my hands behind my back, led me down the hall and through the steel door into the same room where I had met with Mr. Johnson earlier in the day.

Dad was there accompanied by a tall young man that I had occasionally seen in church and around town. Words can't express how glad I was to see the two of them. I recognized the man who was with my father. He was an attorney and I had been told that he was the best lawyer in the county. His name was Tom Ford and I used to deliver his paper every day.

Mr. Ford was somewhat of a legend around our town. He had been a basketball star in high school and then received a basketball scholarship to Virginia Military Institute in Lexington. After his graduation in 1941, he was commissioned as a second lieutenant in the Army, and sent to Fort Knox in Kentucky for training as a tank commander. A few years later, he became a noted war hero. Tom Ford had been awarded not only the Purple Heart, but also two Bronze Stars and the Silver Star as well. I had read all about him in the local paper.

After the war, this decorated veteran had gone to the University of Virginia where he received his law degree before returning to Redbank where he set up his successful law practice.

When Mr. Ford was suddenly thrust into my life, he was the up and coming attorney in the area and was even being talked about as the next county prosecutor. But right now, my dad had secured his services as my defense attorney. It was certainly my lucky day to have Tom Ford on my side.

Mr. Ford (or Tom as he told me to call him), asked me many of the same questions Mr. Johnson had asked previously. But Tom also added many questions of his own. Many of his new questions concerned my pistol. Why had I purchased a pistol? How did I acquire it? Who did I buy the pistol from? Where did I get the ammunition? How many times had I fired the gun? Where did I fire it? But the most importantly, who had I told about the pistol? And had I told anyone where I had hidden it?

To the last series of questions, I answered that I had told only one person about the gun. My best friend, Jack Algood. I had told Jack about purchasing the pistol, but I didn't think I had told him where it was hidden.

"Are you sure you didn't tell him where the gun was stored?" Tom pressed me for an answer.

I pondered the question. "I'm not positive, but I don't think I told him about storing it in the lunch box. I'm not sure whether I did or not."

"Think now," Tom said. "This is very important. Did you happen to mention to anyone at any time where you kept the pistol?"

I searched my memory, trying to recall. "I'm pretty sure that I didn't, but then again, maybe I did. I'll have to think about it and try to remember. If I told anyone, it would have only been Jack Algood." I tried to explain my dilemma. "I'm really confused right now and scared too. I'm just not thinking straight."

"Well, you need to give it some deep thought and we'll cover it again later," he replied. "Now let's talk now about your actions of last night. Give me a minute-by-minute run down of your entire Monday evening. Go slow and try to remember every little thing you did. Take it from supper time until you went to bed."

I tried to recall everything that had happened. "Let's see. I had supper with my parents last night. Mom had fixed pork chops with mashed potatoes and gravy. Oh yeah, we had peas too. I really don't care much for peas." I was rambling, but I didn't want to forget to tell him anything. "We also had rolls and butter and I drank a glass of milk. Mom and dad had coffee, but I don't drink coffee."

"What time was that," Tom asked. "Remember that we're going minute by minute."

I looked over at Dad and continued. "I was late to dinner because I was reading a comic book in the bathroom. It must have been about six-forty when I sat down at the table and we were done eating shortly after seven o'clock."

It was all coming back to me. "I had told Barb, Barb James that is, and Jack Algood that I would pick them up at seven-fifteen at her house. Dad had told me that I could use the family car so I drove over to get them. But when I got there Jack still hadn't arrived, so Barb and I left without him."

"You're doing really well, Jack" Tom commended me as he continued to write on his pad of paper. "What did you and Barb do next?"

"We drove into town and stopped at the Sweet Shop to see if Jack might be there, but he wasn't. So we just had a Coke and then left to drive around for awhile."

"Go on," Tom urged me.

"Well," I hesitated looking over at Dad and then continuing, "Barb suggested that we drive up on the hill to a spot that we both liked."

"What hill would that be?" my attorney inquired.

"All of us call it Breezy Summit. I don't know its real name. A lot of the kids go up there to...uh, uh, look at the moon," I stuttered. It was the first time that I had ever admitted in front of my dad to parking anywhere with a girl.

"Its okay, Jack," Tom assured me. "We used to call it Breezy Summit too when I was in high school. And yes, we used to park up there with our girlfriends. There's no reason to be embarrassed."

Dad just sat there looking me in the eye and giving me a reassuring smile that really did a lot more for me than a lot of words.

Tom continued with his questioning. "How long did you spend up there? And what time did you drop Barb off at her house?"

"I guess we left the hill right after nine o'clock because I got her home right at nine-fifteen. And it would have been just before nine-thirty when I got to my house." I paused trying not to forget anything. "I remember the time because mom was listening to the radio and the Lawrence Welk Show was just coming on. I listened to it with her for a little while and then went upstairs, took a shower and got into bed about ten-fifteen."

"Then the next thing I recall, it was morning and the doorbell was ringing," I concluded. "And then there was the loud knocking."

Tom stopped me there and said we would continue later. "You're doing fine," he assured me. "Try to remember about the pistol. That's really a big thing." He left the room and I had a short time to talk alone with my dad.

"Son, I believe you're telling the truth and that you had nothing to do with the murder of Dr. Adams," my dad told me. "I know that you're a good boy and would never do anything like that. I'm going to get you out of here just as soon as possible. By now you certainly know that you should never have bought that gun, don't you? That was very wrong."

"Yes, Dad. I think I knew it was wrong at the time. But I only fired it one time. When I did, the pistol sort of exploded and burnt my right hand. I never fired it again. Really, I only fired it one time." I felt tears well up in my eyes as I tried to explain.

I think I saw some tears in my dad's eyes too as he said, "Jack, you know that your mom and I really love you and will stand by you in this."

"Yes, Dad, I know that," I responded. "But I guess that I really needed to hear you say it. I love you and mom so much and I would never do anything to make you ashamed of me. I'm so sorry."

Dad stood up and I knew his time with me was coming to an end. "I know that you love us, Jack, and so does your mother. Try not to worry. The whole church is praying for you and the new associate pastor, Max MacCormick, called and said that he would be coming by to see you later today. But right now I must go before they lock me up in here with you."

As soon as Dad left, the jailer came in, put on the handcuffs and led me off to the same cell I had been in before. It wasn't any better than when I had left it. In a few minutes the guard returned with a stack of prison clothes and told me to strip and change into them right down to my underwear and shoes. Not only was I going to lose my clothes, but I was starting to feel a loss of my identity too.

I changed into the faded blue denim bib overalls and the blue shirt, both of which were way too big for me. Stenciled across the back of the shirt in big black letters were the words "Shawnee County Jail." Even the overalls had a "P" (for prisoner) stenciled on the seat of the pants. The shoes were old brown high tops with no laces, the kind we called brogans. I hadn't even been given any socks to wear with the shoes.

As I got dressed, I realized that on the outside I looked like a convict. My innocence seemed to be hidden under my new jailhouse clothes. I could only hope that people wouldn't judge by my outward appearance but would look at my heart.

CHAPTER 7

THE GIFT

That afternoon about four o'clock the associate pastor from the church stopped by the jail to see me. Well, I guess it was four o'clock because I had heard the clock on the courthouse tower chime four times just a few minutes before he arrived. I didn't know the exact time because my watch had been taken from me. The jailer let the pastor into my cell and then locked the door behind us. I was happy that the guard didn't stay to listen in on our conversation.

Rev. Max MacCormick introduced himself as we shook hands. He was a nice looking fellow about thirty years old with reddish hair. I was surprised to see that he was dressed in slacks and a sport shirt, not at all what I expected to see a minister wear. Not a black suit and tie, but only very ordinary clothes. He was even wearing grey suede shoes. I liked him immediately and was glad that he had come.

He told me to call him Max that he said was short for Maxwell. Max had only been in Redbank for a couple of weeks and hadn't even been formally introduced in church yet. Since Pastor Williams, our senior pastor, was attending a statewide church meeting in the capital for a few days, Max was filling in for him. Probably he never expected one of his first duties was going to be visiting the county jail.

Max seemed to be a really sincere person who was obviously deeply concerned for my welfare. He had a nice smile and I felt really comfortable talking to him.

"I've brought you a gift," he told me. "This is something that will really help you while you're here in this place."

The gift was a small Bible with a black leather cover. I had never had a Bible of my own. A few times I had carried my mother's Bible to a youth meeting at the church, but I had never really read anything from the Bible. I will admit that I had tried to read the Bible, but it never made any sense to me. There were too many "thees" and "thous" and other big words to stumble over. But this new Bible I held in my hand seemed different. Or perhaps I was different. Somehow I felt like I would understand it now.

Max suggested that I read the Gospel of John, which he informed me was the fourth book in the New Testament. He then proceeded to read the first couple of verses aloud and put a red ribbon there to mark the place

Then he asked me a very important question, "Have you ever received Jesus into your life and asked Him to forgive all your sins?"

"No, sir," I replied honestly. "I've never even thought about it. I don't even know how to go about doing it. I'm not very religious."

"Well, Jack, this is something that every person must do if they expect to find their way to heaven some day. And religion actually has nothing to do with it. It's a personal decision."

I must admit that I was getting a little confused by the conversation. "But, Max, I am a Christian. I know I'm a Christian because my parents are both Christians and I joined the church when I was twelve along with a lot of other kids."

Max smiled as he spoke these words. "God doesn't have any grandchildren. He only has children. You won't become a Christian just because your parents are Christians." Max paused for a minute to let his words sink in. "And going into a church won't make you a Christian anymore than going into a barn will make you a cow."

I had to laugh when I heard him say that. The simple things Max was telling me were starting to make sense.

"Your parents can't take away your sins and neither can going to church remove them," Max continued. "Only Jesus can take away your sins."

I had never heard anyone talk about things like this before and I commented on that to Max. He seemed surprised and asked me if anyone had ever told me that I needed to be born again.

"Not that I remember," I replied. "I don't think that I ever heard anything about that in church or Sunday school."

"I can see that there is a lot of work to be done here in Redbank," Max stated. "What we have talked about is very important and you need to give it some very deep thought, Jack."

As he stood up to leave, he told me that he would be back for another visit soon. Max also reminded me again to start reading the Bible and then he bowed his head and prayed for me, asking God's peace to rest upon me and to keep me safe and free from harm. It sounded like Max was actually talking to God, and in the midst of my inner turmoil, I did sense a quiet peace come over me as he prayed.

Max was gone and I was alone in my cell again. I thought about what he had said. No one had ever confronted me about spiritual matters before and I had to admit that his words had really left me with something to think about and ponder in my heart.

About six o'clock the jailer appeared at my cell again, this time with a tray that he shoved through a slit in the door saying, "Here's your dinner."

I realized that I hadn't had any breakfast or lunch and I was famished. However, I took one look at the food on the tray and almost lost my appetite. There was a thick piece of fried Spam, some pork and beans and a slice of dry bread. But I realized just how hungry I really was and decided to eat what had been provided. The only utensil on the tray was a large spoon. I felt really funny about eating the Span with a spoon, but I didn't have any choice. It was either the spoon or my fingers.

There was also a cup of black coffee with my meal. I don't drink coffee and don't even like the smell of coffee, so I just pushed it over to the side of the tray. The Spam was bad enough. I certainly wasn't going to wash it down with coffee.

That Tuesday evening passed slowly without incident. I had never felt so alone in my entire life. At exactly nine-thirty the lights suddenly went out, so I laid the Bible beside my cot and stretched out on the dirty mattress. I was totally alone in the dark with nothing but my thoughts for company. There was no pillow for my head and no blanket to wrap around me for comfort and warmth. I felt totally exposed there on the bare cot. It was going to be a long night.

As I lay there, my thoughts went back to my visits with Tom and Max. I thought long and hard about what the two men had said to me that afternoon. I also considered the charges that had been brought against me. I knew that there was no truth in them, but I wondered if Mr. Ford could prove me innocent. If not, what did the future hold for me? A picture of a gallows and hangman's noose appeared in my mind's eye. I had heard that was the punishment for murder. Could I be facing something like that? The answer came to me quickly: Yes I probably could. But how could I prove my innocence?

That night in the cold cell, I did something that I had never really done before. I prayed. Oh sure, I had been raised to say my prayers. Every night when I got into bed, I would repeat the prayer I had learned as a child. "Now I lay me down to sleep. I pray the Lord my soul to keep." And then I would continue, "God bless mom and dad" . . . and finish off the prayer with a whole list of relatives. And of course, I never forgot to add my dog, Spot.

But was that really praying? I wasn't so sure any more. Somehow there in the darkness of the jail, I realized that real prayer was when you revealed the deep thoughts of your heart to God and then listened for Him to reply.

That night alone in my cell in the county jail, I opened my heart before God and asked Him to forgive me of all my sin. I prayed that God would not only set me free from my sin, but that He would also set me free from the charges that had been brought against me. I pleaded with Him to help me prove my innocence and to give Tom Ford wisdom as to how to handle my case.

I must have prayed for hours. I prayed that God would give mom and dad peace and wouldn't allow them to worry. And I also prayed for Barb and Anne and especially for Jack Algood. When I thought that I had covered everything, I closed my first real prayer with these words that came into my mind, "I ask all this in the wonderful name of Jesus Christ the Lord. Amen."

Suddenly a wonderful peace came over me and I had the assurance that this whole situation was going to work out just fine. I must have drifted off into a restful sleep because I didn't wake up until Wednesday morning when the jailer began banging on the bars of the cell.

The guard didn't say good morning or anything. He just handed me a toothbrush already spread with toothpaste and informed me that the water would only be on for the next ten minutes. He added that I had better hurry up and use the toilet while there would be water available to flush it.

"I'll be coming with your breakfast in a few minutes so brush your teeth and get moving," he stated as he turned to leave.

There really wasn't much choice but to fall in with the jail routine, even though I didn't like it. And I didn't like breakfast either. Again there was a greasy slice of fried Spam, some kind of mush that vaguely resembled oatmeal, a chunk of dry bread and of course, another cup of coffee. I asked if I could possibly have milk instead of coffee.

The jailer laughed out loud at my request, however he did consent to let me have a cup of water. It was a small victory, but I was learning that even little things can be a blessing. I remembered to thank God for my food, even though it was Spam.

CHAPTER 8

JAILBIRD

My attorney arrived around ten o'clock on Wednesday morning with the news that he had finally been able to reach Judge Raymond J. Hightower, the county judge, on the phone. The judge was in Richmond attending the annual meeting of the Virginia Synod of the Presbyterian Church with Pastor Williams and had been very difficult to locate. The two men weren't scheduled to return to Redbank until Friday, but Tom had been able to persuade Judge Hightower to return a day early. He would be coming back tomorrow. This meant that I would only have to remain in jail for one more day instead of two.

Tom had already told me that when the judge returned I would be brought before the bench for arraignment. At that time the charges that had been made against me would be officially read.

"If Judge Hightower decides to hold you over for trial, I intend to ask for bail to be set at that time," Tom informed me. "I really don't believe that the case will actually come to trial and I can't see any reason that the request for bail shouldn't be granted."

I certainly wasn't looking forward to spending another full day behind bars, but Tom seemed so confident that I would soon be free that I was encouraged by his words. Another day in jail meant another cold night, so I asked Tom if he could get me a blanket.

"That shouldn't be too much of a problem," he answered. "Is there anything else you want?"

I knew exactly what I wanted. I felt like I was starving and the thought of eating Spam for another day was almost unbearable. "Could you bring me a hamburger from Ozzie's. The food in this place is really terrible. You can't even imagine how bad it is."

Ozzie's Cafe was a little restaurant in town run by an elderly Greek couple who made the best hamburgers and grilled cheese sandwiches in the county. It had always been one of my favorite places to eat.

"Sure, I can take care of that," Tom replied. "Do you want fries to go along with your burger?

My mouth was watering just thinking about it. "Fries would be great. And lots of ketchup on the hamburger. Oh, and while you're at it, maybe you could add a chocolate milkshake to that order."

Tom laughed and said, "Your dad will bring the food when he stops by later. You just stay here and don't go away." I had to smile at his feeble attempt at a joke. I certainly wasn't going anywhere. At least not for another twenty-four hours.

It wasn't too much later that the jailer brought me an old army blanket and also some socks. He seemed willing to stay and talk for a while so I was finally able to ask him where all the other prisoners were since I hadn't heard any voices or noise the entire time I had been in my cell. I was informed that there usually wasn't anyone who was locked up during the week, but that weekends were a little different when the drunks were cleared off the streets. Apparently that was the norm for Redbank, the quiet little town in the Shenandoah Valley.

It was a long, lonely afternoon before my cell was visited again by the guard. He opened my cell door and ordered, "Follow me! You have a visitor."

He then turned and walked down the hall toward the steel door without even putting the cuffs on me. I guessed that he didn't expect me to give him any trouble. Either that or he just plain forgot about them. I was led into the same windowless room where I had been questioned in the beginning by Mr. Johnson, the state's attorney.

I was overjoyed when I saw that my dad was waiting for me. He stood up and gave me a really big hug and told me, "Your mom wanted to come along with me, but I suggested that it would be better if she stayed at home today. I don't want her to have any memory of you here in jail since you're going to be getting out of here very soon now."

His words, plus his hug, did a whole lot to lift my spirits. Or perhaps it was just the smell of the hamburger and fries that were coming from the bag on the table. Dad and I sat down together as I literally devoured the food he had brought. I'm not sure that anything had ever tasted that good.

When I had finally finished the last crumb and drained every drop of the milkshake from the cup, Dad stood up from the table and faced me. Somehow I knew that we were going to have a very serious conversation.

"Son," Dad began, "I am only going to ask this question once and I know that you will answer truthfully. As far as I know, you have never lied to me about what has happened, but I must hear your answer again."

He paused and then continued, "Did you have anything at all to do with the death of Dr. Adams?"

I looked him straight in the eye and replied, "Honestly, Dad, I had absolutely nothing to do with his death. It was a total surprise when the police came into my room that morning. I didn't even know what they were talking about."

My father breathed a sign of relief. "Your mother and I were convinced that you would have never committed a murder or harmed anyone, but I had to ask you the question directly."

We both sort of relaxed and the tension in the room lifted as we continued talking together. Dad asked me how my meeting had gone with Tom Ford. I was able to assure him that it had gone really well and that I liked Tom and trusted him a lot.

"I talked to Tom this afternoon just before I came over," Dad told me, "and he said to tell you that the judge is on his way back and will be here in the morning. The arraignment should take place about ten o'clock."

It was good to get this information and also to learn that Tom would be bringing me some decent clothes to wear into the courtroom.

"We certainly don't want you to appear looking like some sort of criminal or a common drunk," Dad said with a smile. "You're going to look great and soon this will all be behind us and you'll be back home."

Before he left, my Dad asked me if here was anything I needed. I did have one request. I wanted him to pray for me.

My Dad reached out to me and took me in his arms. "I thought you would never ask." Then he prayed a wonderful prayer that was straight from his heart. He asked the Lord to watch over me and keep me safe from all harm. "And, dear God," he concluded, "please keep my son free from all suspicion and gossip that might arise from what has happened."

It had been wonderful to have my father pray for me. "Thanks for praying, Dad." I paused before adding, "I would have never thought about anything like suspicion and gossip. Are people talking about me?"

"Well, you know how people are," Dad replied. "There's plenty of talk around town already and I don't want you to be subjected to any of it. Idle tongues do have a tendency to wag, you know."

He started to leave and then suddenly turned back to give me another big hug and a kiss on the cheek. I don't believe that my Dad had kissed me since I was about twelve years old. Surprisingly, I really liked it.

CHAPTER 9

THE ARRAIGNMENT

It was the start of another day. As usual, the jailer arrived at my cell promptly at six-thirty Thursday morning with the now familiar toothbrush and paste and informed me that the water would be on in a minute. And once again I was told that he would be back with my breakfast shortly. The daily routine never varied in the Redbank jail.

When I finished brushing my teeth, I found myself wondering who had used this toothbrush last. But it was too late to be concerned about things like that because my breakfast tray was being delivered. Same old thing with one exception. There was a big tin cup of cold milk instead of coffee. I remembered to thank the guard when he came to collect the tray.

Just as the courthouse clock was striking nine, Tom Ford arrived bringing with him some of my own clothes including clean underwear and a pair of shoes for me to wear to the arraignment. I knew that if I had to return to my cell after the hearing, I would once again be back into jail clothes, but I was believing that wouldn't happen. It was good to get dressed and no longer look like a criminal. I almost felt like Jack White again.

While I was getting into my clothes, Tom told me that he had been asking around town about the events of Monday night. He had checked out what I had told him, paying particular attention to the times that I had mentioned, and even had talked with Barb James and her parents. They had confirmed everything that I had said.

Tom did add that Mr. James had been surprised to learn that his daughter had been parked on Breezy Summit, a place with a rather sordid reputation. But at least that was out in the open and Barb and I were being truthful about everything that we had done that night. Apparently both Barb and her mother were going to be at the courthouse this morning in case they were needed to appear before the judge.

Tom looked at his watch and said, "It's about time for us to go over to the court house. The deputy will be here in just a minute to take you to the arraignment. You look good, Jack. Don't worry. It's going to be fine."

He had no sooner finished speaking when the deputy arrived, put cuffs on me and escorted us on the short walk to the courthouse and up the stairs to the hearing room.

As we were about to enter into the room, I noticed Barb and her mother coming up the stairs. I would normally have waved, but the handcuffs prevented me from doing so. All I could do was smile. Happily, Barb smiled back at me. An encouraging sign, I thought.

To my surprise, this was not a fancy courtroom like you see in the movies. There were just three tables set up in the room. One was directly opposite the door we had just entered and the two others were set up with one on the left and one on the right. Tom motioned me to the left side, telling me that the other table was for the state's attorney.

Shortly after we took our seats, Aaron Johnson, the gentleman who had questioned me at the jail, came in with two other men. They took their seats at the other table and the deputy stationed himself outside of the door. A few minutes later Judge Hightower came into the room and sat down alone at his table. I had been delivering his newspaper for two years so I recognized him immediately.

The judge was the first to speak. Looking directly at Mr. Johnson, he asked, "What is this business that is so important that you have called me back from Richmond?"

"Well, sir," the attorney stated, "as I told you on the phone, Dr. Andrew Adams was shot and killed about midnight on Monday night in that little barn in back of his house as he was parking his car. The state police have established that someone was apparently hiding in the corncrib that is built into the barn. It has a door from the outside and another door opening into the barn."

Mr. Johnson looked down briefly at his notes. "As the doctor got out of his car, someone came through the crib door into the barn and shot the doctor at very close range. The bullet entered behind his right ear and exited his head over the left eye. Dr. Adams was dead before he hit the ground. The slug was recovered from a rafter above the front door of the barn." The attorney continued, "Whoever shot Dr. Adams also robbed him of approximately one thousand dollars."

Turning, he pointed his finger directly at me. "And I believe that's the person sitting right here in this room."

"What evidence do you have to support your assumptions, Aaron?" asked the judge.

"Let me back up a little first," Mr. Johnson began. "Mrs. Adams phoned the police shortly after midnight saying that her husband had been shot and was lying beside his car in what she called the garage. I call it a barn. She was in a terrible state of mind when she called. The police went immediately to the house and found Dr. Adams just as his wife had described."

The attorney continued summarizing the events of that terrible night. "I was called to the scene of the crime about one-thirty and interviewed Mrs. Adams the best that I could under the circumstances. She really wasn't in any condition to add much information. Apparently she heard her husband's car pull into the drive at five minutes after twelve and then heard a loud bang about two minutes later. When her husband didn't come into the house, she sent their live-in maid, a girl named Missie Williams, to investigate. The maid came running back screaming that the doctor was dead."

Looking down at his notes, he continued the presentation. "I then spoke at some length with their daughter Anne and found it to be very enlightening. It seems as though she had been dating this young fellow seated here since October. His name is actually John, but everyone always calls him Jack."

The judge interrupted saying, "I know Jack. He used to be my paper boy and always got my paper there right on time."

"I'm glad to hear that, Judge," Mr. Johnson responded. "But let me tell you what I learned from Anne. She told me that she had recently been pregnant and when her father found out, he had interrupted the pregnancy. Those were her exact words, interrupted the pregnancy. She said that her father was absolutely furious with Jack and said he was going to deal with him."

The judge leaned forward listening intently as the story unfolded. "To keep Anne from seeing Jack after the abortion, her father had taken the family to The Homestead in Hot Springs for an entire week. Anne told me that it was over two weeks before she managed to get word to Jack about her father's threat and told him about the abortion that had been performed."

Mr. Johnson then added these incriminating words that Anne had spoken during his interview with her: "I knew that Jack would be upset over what had happened, but I didn't think he would do anything like this. I can't believe that Jack killed my father."

No wonder they thought I had killed Dr. Adams. It was no secret that I had been seeing Anne. The police had jumped to the conclusion that I was the Jack who had had gotten Anne pregnant and that I was the Jack who had killed Dr. Adams. Everything pointed to me as the murderer.

But Mr. Johnson wasn't done yet with his report of the investigation. "Based on the information obtained during my interview with Mrs. Adams and with her daughter Anne, a warrant was secured from the Justice of the Peace for the arrest of Jack White. Two policemen were then dispatched to the White residence on Jackson Street about seven-thirty this past Tuesday morning. Mr. White, the boy's father, came to the door and when he was shown the warrant, allowed the officers to enter the premises. They went directly to the room where Jack was sleeping and arrested him for the murder of Dr. Adams. He was then taken to the jail and I was called to conduct the interrogation."

"During the course of my conversation with him, Jack told me that he had purchased an old pistol from someone named Norman Smithers who supposedly lives up on the mountain."

I took a deep breath knowing that some pretty damning evidence was going to be brought up about the gun. How I regretted making that impulsive purchase last June. But what was done was done.

"In our search of the White residence we found this pistol," Mr. Johnson said holding up the gun. "As you can see it's a .38-caliber Smith & Wesson with a five inch barrel, commonly called a Police Special. We discovered it wrapped in a piece of burlap hidden in an old lunch box in the Whites' garage. A box of shells was also found which originally contained twenty-five cartridges. Twenty were still in the box and three more unfired cartridges remained in the cylinder along with two discharged shell casings. One space in the cylinder was empty and was also cracked, as was the first one containing a spent shell casing."

Mr. Johnson placed the gun back on the table and picked up an official looking paper. "We sent the pistol and the box of cartridges over to the police lab on Tuesday morning. This is their report that I have in my hand. Their examination shows that the pistol has two defective chambers, both of which are cracked. One chamber was found to be empty and two others held the discharged shell casings. All of the shells and shell casings in the pistol have John White's fingerprints on them, however the weapon has been wiped clean. No fingerprints were found on either the weapon or on the lunch box. This report and the other evidence here is available for your inspection," the judge was informed.

"After a somewhat lengthy interrogation at the jail, John White was read the standard arresting warrant which he signed. The warrant charged him with the premeditated murder of Dr. Andrew Adams. I have the signed warrant here on the table. Would you like to see it?" Mr. Johnson asked Judge Hightower holding up the paper.

The judge indicated that he did not. "Is there anything else?"

It seemed to me that the attorney raised his voice as he spoke these words. "I just want to say that all the evidence points to John White here as the guilty party and we believe he should be remanded over for trial as an adult on the charge of murder in the first degree."

Finally Mr. Johnson had finished speaking and sat down at his table. Now it was our turn. I wondered what Tom Ford could possibly say to prove my innocence in the light of all the evidence that seemed to be stacked against me.

It was a relief when the judge turned to Tom and asked, "What do you have to say in answer to all of this?"

Tom stood to his feet and began to speak, "Judge, we will agree with several of the statements Mr. Johnson made in his presentation. Firstly, we confirm that the pistol is Jack's gun. He bought it last June from a Mr. Norman Smithers whose address is unknown. And Jack has also admitted that he purchased the shells for the gun at Mr. James' hardware store a day or two later using the name of Jed Martin. We do not dispute the fact that the gun used in the murder was Jack's gun. However, we deny empathically that Jack had anything to do with the unfortunate death of Dr. Adams. I trust that you have no objection if I call my client Jack."

"I really have no problem with that," Judge Hightower replied. "You may continue using that name."

"Thank you, sir," Tom responded and continued on with my defense. "I have creditable witnesses waiting outside of this court room who will verify that Jack was nowhere near the scene when this terrible incident took place. Plus there are numerous people in this town who will testify that such an act is totally out of character for this young man."

There was a pause as my attorney looked down at his notes before resuming. "Now I realize that the doctor's own daughter told Mr. Johnson about how upset her father was with Jack over her pregnancy. But I would ask Mr. Johnson to consider this: Was Anne Adams talking about Jack White during that interview or was she talking about some other person named Jack? I believe there is a definite question as to the true identity of the person Anne made reference to on the night of the murder. I further believe that Mr. Johnson has jumped to his conclusion prematurely."

Tom then concluded with these words, "Based on this, I respectfully request that all charges against my client be dropped and that he be released immediately."

A few minutes passed before the judge responded. Finally he said, "Mr. Ford, you have brought up some points that definitely have to be considered. However, there remains sufficient evidence to take this matter to the people. Therefore I am holding John C. White over for trial as an adult on the charges before us today. Bail will be set at the sum of fifteen hundred dollars to be paid in cash to the county clerk. If you hurry, you can take care of that before the clerk goes for lunch."

Tom looked over at me and smiled. I wasn't sure yet how the judge's ruling was going to affect me, but I thought I was going to get to go home.

The judge wasn't done speaking however, and had more information to add to his decision. "Usually I like to have a month or more between the arraignment and the trial, but considering how close we are to Christmas, I believe that both sides can have their cases ready to be heard by a jury on Monday morning, December tenth at ten o'clock. The trial should take no more that a week at the most. I realize that both of you would like to have more than ten days to prepare, but you are both competent attorneys so let's get this thing all wrapped up before Christmas."

The judge was quickly bringing the session to a close. "There being no further matters before us today, I am ready for my lunch. You are dismissed." With that, Judge Raymond Hightower stood to his feet and marched out of the hearing room leaving both lawyers standing there looking at each other, wondering if they could possibly meet the judge's deadline of ten days.

Tom Ford turned to me and said, "Let's get you back across the alley to the jail and then I'll get your dad and the money for the bail. We need to get you out of this place and home as quickly as possible."

As we left the courtroom, the state's attorney was whispering to his associates with a very puzzled look on his face. In the hallway I noticed that Barb James and her mother were sitting on a bench. Both of them looked at me and smiled as I passed by. Glancing over my shoulder, I mouthed to Barb, "Call you later."

Outside of the courthouse, as we hurried toward the jail, I asked Mr. Ford, "What just happened in there? I really didn't understand everything that the judge was saying."

As we walked along together, Tom attempted to explain the current situation to me. "The judge set your bail at only fifteen hundred dollars, which is a very small sum considering the charge against you. To me this means a couple of things, both of which are good for us. First, he seems to believe that you are trustworthy and won't attempt to leave the area. Secondly, he is pretty sure that the evidence presented will not stand up against you in court. Plus I think that the judge really likes you, Jack." Tom grinned at me and added, "It's a good thing that you didn't toss his newspaper in the bushes every day."

Back at the jail, I was once again locked in my cell. But it wasn't long before the jailer came and led me into that windowless room where I found my dad and Tom were waiting. They both had big smiles on their faces.

"You're free to go," Dad told me. "Everything has been taken care of and you've been released."

Tom had a few final words for me. "I'm sure you realize that you are not to leave town under any circumstances. I'll phone you after we have all had some lunch. We still have a lot to talk about together."

Turning to my father, Tom said, "Mr. White, you can take your son home."

To this my dad replied, "Thank You, Lord!" And then he took me by the arm and led me out to the car. I was a free man. I was going home.

CHAPTER 10

HOME AGAIN

I never realized how good Mom's cooking was until I sat down at the table for lunch after I arrived home. Perhaps I really shouldn't call it lunch. My mother must have spent the whole morning preparing a special meal for me. There was fried chicken with mashed potatoes and gravy, along with a big bowl of buttered corn. Mom had even opened one of her jars of corn that she had canned at the end of summer. The days of eating Spam were quickly forgotten. For dessert was a slice of Mom's famous apple pie and a big glass of cold milk.

"I was supposed to stop on the way home to pick up some ice cream to go with the pie," Dad told me. "But I got so excited about having you in the car with me that I completely forgot."

My mom just couldn't stop kissing me and telling me how much she loved me. Ordinarily I would have been embarrassed by such a show of affection, but I have to admit that I actually liked it. And I also liked it when she told me that the two of them had been praying for me while I was away.

We must have spent an hour sitting at the table over lunch. My parents wanted to know everything that the judge had said and also about the bail that had been set. I was glad to be able to tell them that

Mr. Ford advised me that the money that had been posted as bond would be returned to dad when I showed up for the trial on the tenth of the month. I had told them that I had been instructed not to leave town.

Mom then asked me about school. "You must be pretty far behind in your studies, aren't you?" she asked.

"I expect that I am," I replied. "Probably I need to call Miss Curry and ask about getting my assignments."

Miss Amanda Curry was our class sponsor and I knew that she would do everything she could to help me catch up with my work. To be honest, I really hadn't given much thought to school while I was locked up in the jail. It was like I had been living in another world. But now I was back home and life was slowly getting back to normal.

"I'll phone Miss Curry just as soon as she gets home from school and see what I should do about my classes," I remarked.

Actually there was someone else I wanted to talk to a lot more than my teacher and that was Barb. It really meant a lot to me that she had actually come to the courthouse to vouch for me. I realized that I needed to tell her and her mom just how much I appreciated them being there.

I waited until three o'clock when I knew that school was over and she would be back home to make the phone call. I took the phone on its long cord into my room and called Barb.

Redbank only had four telephone operators and I wondered which one would be on duty. It turned out to be Goldie. I recognized her voice as soon as I heard her say, "Number, please."

"Hi, Goldie," I responded. "Would you please connect me with the James residence."

"Oh, Jack! It's you! I'm so glad that you're out of jail."

Obviously Goldie had recognized my voice too. Telephone operators in small towns knew everyone and everything, so I wasn't at all surprised that she was aware of what had been going on.

"I couldn't believe it when I heard that they had arrested you," Goldie said quickly. "It's so terrible about Dr. Adams. I was the operator on duty the night when Mrs. Adams called the police to report the murder. Now don't you tell anyone, but I listened in on the conversation to hear what had happened."

I interrupted her. "Goldie, we can talk about that later, but right now I want to speak with Barbara. Could you please ring her for me?"

"Sure, I'll do that right now, Jack. And by the way, good luck."

I thought that Goldie was finally going to put me through, but she still had more to report before completing the connection.

"Incidentally, did you hear that Mr. Algood reported his car missing on Tuesday morning? And that's not all. Later the maid at the Adams' house, Missie somebody, called the police and told them that Anne was missing." Goldie kept rambling on and on.

I thought that she would never stop talking and at this point I was getting really annoyed. "Goldie, just put my call through to Barb, will you?"

She actually sounded apologetic. "Sure, I'm ringing the number now."

The phone only rang twice before Mrs. James answered, "Hello. This is the James' residence."

"Hi there, Mrs. James. This is Jack White. May I please speak with Barb?" And then I remembered how grateful I was about her visit to the courthouse and added, "Thanks so much for coming this morning with Barb to the hearing."

"It was no problem. And Jack, we want you to know that we believe in you and are standing behind you. Oh, here's Barbara now."

Barb sounded excited when she started talking, "I've been waiting for your call ever since I got back from school. All the kids are talking about you and how you were arrested and put in jail."

"I'll bet they are. Bad news travels fast," I replied. "And I have some news too. Have you heard anything about Anne being missing? Or that Mr. Algood's car is gone? Goldie just told me about it when I was calling you. These telephone operators seem to always know everything that's happening in town."

I continued on without even giving Barb a chance to make a comment. "Goldie also told me she took the call when the police were contacted about Dr. Adams death."

Suddenly I realized that I wasn't giving Barb much of a chance to say anything. "How are you doing, Barb? I really missed you so much."

"I'm feeling a lot better now that I know you're out of that horrible jail. It must have been terrible in there," she commented.

It felt so good to be talking with her. Barb was the only person who really understood the complexity of the situation I was facing. I needed her like I had never needed her before.

"Believe me, I'm glad to finally be out. Yes, it was awful in there and the food was horrible. I really thought I would never be released."

"Do you know what I think?" Barb asked suddenly. "I believe that Jack and Anne have run off together. And I think that the reason Mr. Algood's car is missing is that Jack took it. What do you think?"

It was an obvious conclusion. "You're probably right, Barb. Did you talk to Anne after last Monday night when her dad was killed?"

"I tried to phone her several times on Tuesday evening, but I couldn't get through. I guess they were notifying people and making funeral arrangements. This is a real mess," Barb replied.

"But I want you to know this, Jack," she continued. "I am absolutely certain that you didn't have anything at all to do with Dr. Adams' death. No matter what people are saying, I'm standing by you. I want you to know that I'll do whatever is needed to help prove your innocence."

I was really touched by her comments. "Gee, thanks Barb. When can I see you? Tonight maybe? Do your parents have any objections to you still going out with me? I don't think I should be driving right now, but we could take a walk or something. Can we get together?"

"I'll ask my mom. Hold on."

She was only gone a minute or two and then she was back on the line. "Mom says it's okay with her. How about seven o'clock?"

"Great," I responded. "Dress warm because it's really cold outside. We could be going to get some snow. See you soon."

I hung up the phone with a sigh of relief. I was going to see Barb again and she believed in me. Things were definitely looking up.

After talking with Barb, I called Miss Curry who told me that she had spoken with all of my teachers and had gotten their assignments for me. She was going to drop them by my house tomorrow. Miss Curry had also talked with the principal and they had decided that it would probably be best if I didn't return to school until after the Christmas holidays when the trial would be over. She also assured me that she knew I wasn't responsible for the death of Dr. Adams and that all the other teachers were also confident that I was innocent of the crime. That was good news.

After dinner that Friday evening, I asked my folks if I could go over to spend some time with Barb. Dad laughed when I asked his permission. "You're asking me if you can go out? That's something you haven't done for a couple of years. Your few days in jail must have done you some good."

I think he must have realized his comment might have hurt my feelings because he quickly added, "I'm just kidding, son. Of course you can go over and see Barb."

As I walked over to the James' house, I tried to stay in the shadows so no one would recognize me and start asking questions. I certainly had already had more than my share of questions over the past few days.

Barb was waiting with her coat on when I arrived at her house and I stuck my head inside to say hello to her folks. Mr. James stood up and came to the door and greeted me with these words, "I want you to know that your job is waiting for you, Jack. Whenever you're ready to meet the public again, just give me a call."

Everyone was being really nice to me and I was starting to overcome the fear that people were going to be looking at me like a criminal. Or even worse, as a murderer.

"Thanks so much, Mr. James. It sure is nice of you to say that. I'll let you know soon when I'm ready to come back to the store."

After telling him to have a nice weekend, Barb and I left the house. It was good to have her walking along at my side again. She wanted to know all about my time in the jail and everything that I had been through since my arrest on Tuesday morning.

I really didn't want to talk about all that had happened, but Barb had a right to know. So I told her all about the gun I had purchased and hidden in the garage and how Anne had told the police about being pregnant and the abortion when she had been questioned.

"And then Anne told the police, and these were her very words, that Jack had gotten her pregnant." I added ending my summary of the events of the past few days. "No wonder they arrested me. They think that I'm the Jack she kept talking about. The Jack who got her pregnant and killed her father."

Barb was silent as she pondered my words. What I wanted to know more than anything else was what her gut feeling was about the Adams murder. Finally I asked her, "What do you think?"

"Well, it's very simple really," Barb stated positively. "Obviously Jack Algood knew where you had hidden the gun. He must have slipped into your garage that night and taken it. Then all he had to do was go to the Adams' house and wait in the barn for Dr. Adams. After he shot Anne's father, he could easily have just returned the gun to its hiding place. No one would have seen him that late at night. Who would ever know?"

I pondered Barb's solution to the mystery. "That may be just the way it happened," I replied. "Then sometime the next day, Jack apparently got in touch with Anne and they ran away together. But where would they have gone?"

Barb thought for a minute before answering, "Anne told me once that she wanted to go to Hagerstown, Maryland where she and Jack could get married. She said that you could get married in Maryland at sixteen without having your parent's consent. I remember her saying that."

We both walked together in silence going over everything in our minds. Finally Barb asked, "Should I should tell someone about what I think could have happened and about my conversation with Anne?"

"You probably should, "I answered. "But talk it over with your folks first and see what they say."

We walked holding hands and talking for about an hour before Barb finally said that she was getting cold and wanted to go home. It had been good to share together and to try to make some sense out of everything. I hadn't put all the pieces of the puzzle together yet, but the picture of what might have happened was becoming clearer in my mind. The only thing I really knew was that I was innocent. All I had to do was prove it.

When I got home, my mother told me that Miss Curry had stopped by and dropped off my books and some instructions from my teachers. I sat down with my folks and chatted for a bit before kissing them goodnight and going up to shower. What a luxury to have a warm shower, my first since the arrest. My own bed was waiting for me with clean sheets and blankets and a soft pillow. And I was going to sleep in clean pajamas instead of dirty underwear.

Before closing my eyes, I talked with the Lord. "Dear God, I thank You for getting me out of that horrible jail. And I thank You for sending Max MacCormick by the jail to talk with me. He really opened my eyes to a lot of spiritual things. Bless him and my mom and dad and Barb and her folks too. And also watch over Jack Algood and Anne Adams wherever they might be tonight. And if it's not asking too much, please let the truth come out about Dr. Adams' murder. Thank You in Jesus' name.

Snuggling down under the covers, I had a good night's sleep and woke up refreshed on Saturday morning, wondering what the new day would bring.

CHAPTER 11

PUZZLE PIECES

It was nearly eight o'clock when I woke up to the smell of frying bacon. After brushing my teeth with my very own toothbrush and once more taking a nice hot shower, I dressed in jeans, a "Red Raider" sweatshirt and my sneakers. When I went down to breakfast, I discovered that mom had once more gone overboard. She not only had country bacon, sliced really thick the way I like it, but also a platter of soft fried eggs along with a huge pile of pancakes with real maple syrup. It was almost like being in heaven. There were also pitchers of both cold milk and fresh orange juice.

Mom watched as I poured myself a large glass of orange juice and then helped myself to four eggs and six hotcakes.

"Do you think that will be enough to hold you until lunch time?" Mom asked with a twinkle in her eye.

"If not, I can always have a piece of that apple pie left over from last night," I replied with a laugh.

My mother was relaxed and in good spirits. "Well, now I am certain that a day or two on lay-away hasn't taken your appetite away from you."

Yes, it was good to be home. I was almost able to forget my arrest and the time I had spent in the jail.

However, as I was devouring mom's great cooking, I was brought back to reality when she mentioned that Tom Ford had called. "You were in the shower so I didn't want to bother you. He wants to come by around eleven and I told him I thought that would be fine. Is that any problem?"

"That sounds great," I answered. "I don't have any plans for today and I really do want to talk to Tom. We didn't have much time yesterday when the hearing was over."

Looking around I realized that I hadn't seen my Dad this morning. "Where's Dad today?" I inquired.

"He's just gotten out of the shower so I would guess that he's shaving right now," Mom told me. "And speaking of shaving, didn't you forget something this morning?"

I ran my hand over my face feeling the obvious growth of whiskers. "When I smelled the bacon cooking, I guess I forgot all about shaving. I'll take care of it later. I want to talk with Dad when he comes down for breakfast."

I sure did appreciate home a lot more than I had last week. Everything seemed so special. Even the air smelled fresher and the sun seemed brighter. And it sure was good to be back with my family. I don't think I had ever realized before how much they really meant to me.

I remained at the table with Dad as he ate his breakfast and we had a long talk together about everything that had happened.

"We saved the newspapers from the past few days," Dad informed me. "I think you should take a look and see what the press is making of this whole affair. There have been reporters nosing around up here from Richmond and Washington. One even came from Baltimore and several others from Harrisonburg, Staunton and Charlottesville."

Dad paused to take another sip of coffee and then continued. "Dr. Adams had an excellent reputation as a physician and was well known throughout the entire area, so people are very interested in this incident. And did you know that this is the first murder in Redbank since the Civil War? It's been a very peaceful little town up until now," he added.

I watched as my father once again lifted the cup to his lips. "And unfortunately, Jack, you are right in the middle of all of this. I really think it would be best if you stayed close to home for the next few days. Those newspaper people are going to be all over downtown looking for someone to interview. You don't need that right now."

My father was a wise man and I really needed his wisdom right now. "I'll stay right here. Anyway, Mr. Ford is coming by to see me at eleven o'clock. Didn't Mom tell you?"

My dad smiled. "I guess it slipped her mind. Probably she was so busy cooking for two starving guys like us that she just forgot to mention it."

Tom Ford arrived right on schedule and mom suggested that we talk in the living room where there was a fire going. Not only was it warmer there, but there would be no interruptions. As we got seated, Tom asked me if I had read any of the papers yet. Since all I had done was glance at them, I hadn't read anything in particular.

"That's good," Tom replied. "It really may be best if you don't spend much time reading the papers right now because some of these articles paint a pretty grim picture of the situation. Newspapers seem to take special delight in printing the bad side of the news."

Mr. Ford opened his briefcase and took out a lot of papers. He had laid out a precise timeline starting on Monday morning that ran through Tuesday morning. Tom asked me to fill it in as best I could minute by minute. I searched my memory to be sure I didn't forget anything. The timeline seemed to be very important to the case.

When I had finished making a few corrections and additions, my attorney began to fill me in on what he had learned about Dr. Adams' movements during the same timeframe.

It seems as though Dr. Adams played poker at the Antler Club that evening. It was a weekly game and some of the men that had been there said that Dr. Adams was the big winner as usual. The doctor had left the club with over a thousand dollars in his pocket. His friends had remarked that Dr. Adams was a regular winner and that several years back he had even won a farm over near Monterey. One of the fellows told Tom that he had heard a rumor that Dr. Adams had a woman stashed there at the farm.

"However, that's probably just a poker rumor," Tom reminded me. "You can't believe everything that you hear."

"But back to the timeline," Tom said looking down at his paper. "His friends said that Dr. Adams left the club about 11:50. It's just a fifteen-minute drive from there to his house. I timed it yesterday just to be sure," Tom advised me. "That would have the doctor arriving just at the time Mrs. Adams told the police, five minutes past midnight. If we allow two minutes for him to park his car in the barn that means that the murder would have taken place at 12:07 in the morning. Well, give or take a minute."

Tom leaned forward toward me as if he was going to share something very special. "At that time you were sound asleep in your bed. Your parents told me that they stayed up until midnight listening to the radio in the living room that is at the foot of the stairs. They assured me that at no time did you come downstairs after going to bed. They are ready to swear under oath that you were at home at that time."

Tom was smiling now. "I think we have a real good case here proving your innocence. Of course there is still the gun. Have you had a chance to think about whether you told Jack Algood about the pistol and where it was hidden in the garage?"

I had spent a lot of time thinking about my conversation with Jack about the gun over the past few days and I was now pretty sure that I had mentioned the hiding place to him.

"I've given it a lot of thought, Tom. I believe that I probably did tell Jack about putting the gun in the old lunch box. He had been in the garage with me many times and knew his way around in there really well. It just goes to figure that if anyone knew where the gun was, it would have been Jack."

My attorney was ready to move on to another subject. "Did you hear that they found Mr. Algood's missing car down in Clifton Forge?" Tom asked.

"I heard that yesterday, but I'm not quite sure where Clifton Forge is," I answered.

"It's just east of Covington and not too far from the West Virginia border. It's a main stop on the C&O Railroad. Clifton Forge is where they hookup or unhook the extra engine that is used to cross the mountains," Tom informed me.

"Do you suppose that Jack and Anne may have gotten on a train there in Clifton Forge?" Again I was putting pieces of the puzzle together in my mind.

"That certainly is a reasonable assumption," Tom remarked. "I expect the police will be checking on all the passenger trains going through Clifton Forge to see if a couple meeting their description boarded a train going either east or west."

I was really concerned about my two friends. "I hope that they find them soon. I imagine that Mrs. Algood is really worried about Jack. He's their only child you know."

Tom nodded his head in agreement. "Yes, I can certainly understand how they might feel. I'm going to go by their house later today to interview both Mr. and Mrs. Algood. I need to ask them if they can give me some information about Jack's movements on Monday evening."

"We need to see how Jack fits into the timeline," Tom added. "From what I can discern, he seems quite likely to be involved in all of this."

Somehow I felt a need to defend Jack. "I hope he's not in any trouble," I told Tom. "He's my best friend. I've known Jack my whole life and he's almost like a brother to me. We didn't have any secrets from each other. I just can't believe that Jack would ever shoot anyone. Could he possibly have killed Dr. Adams?"

My lawyer took a deep breath before answering. "Sometimes people just flip out and do things that they ordinarily would never have done. Often anger can affect people and almost make them go crazy. We'll just have to wait and see how things check out over the next few days."

Tom stood to his feet and put on his overcoat. After he left, I sat there in the living room wondering where Jack and Anne might be. Could Jack have possibly done this horrible thing? I needed to pray about the whole mess and believe that the Lord could help to straighten it out.

CHAPTER 12

SHARING THE SECRET

It was Sunday morning. The window was right beside my bed and I pulled back the curtain to look outside. I was surprised to see that it was snowing.

"It's too early for snow," I thought. And then I realized that it was the second of December. Of course it could snow. In the past we had some really big snows in December.

As I lay there in bed, I thought back over the events of the past week or so. Could this really be happening? Was it possible that I was really involved in this unbelievable situation or was it all just a bad dream? The arrest, the jail cell, the courthouse, the hearing. I was awake but the nightmare hadn't ended.

We always went to church on Sunday morning and I knew my parents expected me to come downstairs wearing a dress shirt and tie. But I just couldn't bear the thought of having everyone in the church turn to look at me as we walked down the aisle to our usual pew in the third row. Not today.

My mother was very understanding when I went down to breakfast and explained my apprehension to her.

"Perhaps it would be better if you stayed home today," she agreed. "Maybe the new associate pastor could come by later and spend some time with you."

I breathed a sigh of relief. "I think that I'd really like that. Max seems to be a great guy."

Mom corrected me, "You mean Pastor MacCormick, don't you?"

"No. He told me I should call him Max when he came to see me in the jail the other day. His first name is really Maxwell," I replied.

"Well, if that's what he told you, then I guess it's okay. I believe Pastor Williams is going to introduce him to the congregation this morning and also give a report of his meeting in Richmond last week," she informed me. "It won't hurt you to miss this one Sunday."

When my parents returned home from church, I think my mother was somewhat surprised to find me sitting in the living room reading the Bible.

"Is that the Bible you're reading?" she asked.

"Max gave it to me when he came to see me the other day. I'm just about to finish reading the book of John. I never understood the Bible before but this is really pretty interesting," I informed her.

Mom smiled. "Our new young associate seems to have already had a positive input into your life. I'm glad that you like him."

As she left the room, she added. "Dinner will be ready in just a few minutes. I made peach cobbler for dessert."

It was about three o'clock when Max knocked on our front door. As I greeted him, I happened to notice his car that was parked out front. It was a bright red MG the most beautiful sports car that I had ever seen. There wasn't another around like it for miles. Max was turning out to be a really cool guy. I had always considered pastors to be pretty stuffy and straight-laced, but not Max.

I could hardly contain my excitement. "Wow! That's a really cool car you're driving. I didn't know that pastors could afford wheels like that."

"Actually I didn't buy it myself," he told me. "My parents gave it to me as a gift when I finished seminary. There is no way that I could have bought it on my salary. I can hardly afford to keep up the insurance payments."

I was overwhelmed. "What a great gift. I can't imagine having a car like that. I've never even ridden in a sports car. Do you think that you could take me for a ride in it sometime?"

"No problem," Max replied. "If this snow stops coming down, maybe we can even do it this afternoon. But right now, let's just spend a little time together. You can bring me up to date on what's been happening."

Mom came into the living room bringing us some of her peach cobbler along with a cup of coffee for Max. After a few minutes, she excused herself, leaving the two of us alone to talk.

"How are you coming along with your Bible reading?" Max asked.

I think he was surprised to hear how many chapters I had already read from the gospel of John.

"Don't overload your plate, Jack," he advised me. "You need to take the Bible in small bites. It's easier to digest that way."

"You talk about the Bible like it's food," I said.

"Well, in a way, it is," Max replied. "It's food for the soul. If you don't feed your spirit, it will never grow and be strong. Your spirit needs food just like your body."

"Hey, I like that," I responded with a smile. "Did they teach you that in seminary?"

"No, not really. It's sort of an analogy that I've come up with over the years," Max told me. "Little word pictures like that can help us understand spiritual things."

And I really was starting to spend time thinking of spiritual things. I felt closer to the Lord than I had ever felt in my whole life.

"Let's talk about you now for a little while," Max said changing the subject. "How are things coming along with the court situation?"

I was relieved to unburden myself to someone. "My dad got me a really great lawyer. His name is Tom Ford and I like him a lot. He reminds me of you because he's so easy to talk to about everything.

Tom says he believes that the case will be dropped as soon as we get it into court."

"When are they going to hold the trial?" Max asked. "I really want to be right there in the court room praying for you."

"The judge scheduled the trial date for December tenth at ten o'clock and said that he wants to have the whole thing settled long before Christmas. So it's not very far away."

"That makes sense," Max replied. "Can I change the subject again? I understand you're good buddies with Jack Algood. Is that right?"

I nodded in agreement. "It sure is. Jack and I have been really good friends since...well, forever. His birthday is just four days before mine. We started school together and still have the same class schedule. And we both play football for the Redbank Red Raiders. I guess you've heard about our team. Jack's a really good halfback. I play end."

"The reason that I asked is that Jack's mother called me yesterday and told me that she is really worried about him," Max said. "Jack is missing, along with his father's car. And not only that, but his mother has learned that Anne Adams is also missing. Mrs. Algood was wondering if perhaps you knew anything that might help the authorities find Jack."

"I was as surprised as anyone else when he I heard Jack was missing," I replied. "Jack and Anne had been dating for a long time until last August when Dr. Adams caught them kissing. Actually, to tell the truth, they were doing more than kissing. Anyway, Anne's father blew his stack and forbid Anne to ever see Jack again. It was really bad."

Looking over at Max, I knew that I could trust him and I made the decision to share with him about the plot we had initiated to allow Jack and Anne to continue their relationship in secret.

"Max, I'm going to tell you something that I've never told anyone before," I began. "After Jack and Anne weren't allowed to see each other anymore, my girl, Barb James, came up with a plan where the two of them could meet and no one would ever know about it. One night in the Sweet Shop where everyone hangs out, Barb and I pretended to have an argument and publicly broke up. Then Jack supposedly started to date Barb and I got permission from Dr. Adams to date Anne. It was like some sort of game that we were playing."

I was trying desperately to make Max understand how this scheme had come about. "You see, what would happen is that I would pick up Anne at her house and Jack would go and pick up Barb at hers. And then the four of us would meet somewhere and switch girls. I know it sounds stupid now, but no one ever suspected anything, not even our parents. We just sort of kept out of sight of everyone."

I paused as I considered how to relate the rest of the story. "It's amazing that no one ever recognized that something was wrong, but our scheme was never discovered. It was all a big lie and terribly deceitful and I'm so sorry that we did it. But it's too late now and there's no way to take it back and make things right."

Max might as well hear the whole sordid truth, so I just keep on talking. "But apparently during this time when Anne and Jack were secretly seeing each other, Jack went too far with Anne and she got pregnant. When her father found out, he did something to end the pregnancy. I'm not exactly sure what. Anyway, he took Anne out of town for a week and when they came back, he wouldn't even allow her to go to school. It was really bad."

It felt good to unload on Max. I ended up by saying, "Then this thing with Dr. Adams happened and now Jack and Anne have disappeared. Barb and I think they may have run away to get married. Tom told me yesterday that the police found Mr. Algood's car in Clifton Forge." I paused and then added, "And that's just about it."

"Is any of this confidential?" Tom asked.

"I don't think so. You might ask Tom Ford. He's my lawyer. Do you know him?" I questioned Max.

"Not yet, but I think that we need to meet. And I also think you need to share with Tom everything that you just told me. It's important that you don't hold anything back or keep anything secret," he advised.

"You want to tell the entire truth. The Bible says that the truth will set you free. And that's what we all want. We want you to be set free."

Looking at his watch, Max said he needed to go. "It looks like it's still snowing," he remarked. "I guess that the ride in my car will have to wait for another day."

Before he left the house, Max prayed with me. And I added my own little P.S. to his prayer asking that the Lord watch over Jack and Anne and keep them safe wherever they might be.

Later that night in bed, I finished the gospel of John and decided to start reading in Matthew. But then remembering what Max had said about eating the Bible in small bites, I laid the Bible aside, turned off the light and after a short prayer went to sleep.

CHAPTER 13

COUNTDOWN

It was countdown time! Just one week remained until the trial would begin on Monday, December tenth at ten o'clock in the morning. I added up the hours in my mind and realized that in exactly one hundred and seventy hours I would be back in the courtroom on trial for murder.

The enormity of that fact hit me like a lead weight. Although I hadn't done anything wrong, I had been charged with the premeditated murder of Anne's father. It was nearly beyond belief. This was something that you only read about in books or saw in the movies. But it was actually happening to me. Me! Jack White!

I knew that I had an excellent attorney in Tom Ford, but had he been able to accumulate enough evidence to convince the jury of my innocence? I could only trust in his ability and in the Lord.

The following week seemed to drag by. I had daily meetings with Tom who always made a point of assuring me that everything looked really good. He had interviewed a lot of people and done a lot of research and he kept telling me to relax. I tried, but I didn't always succeed.

I continued to be concerned about Jack Algood and Anne Adams and kept asking Tom for any recent news. He told me that he had learned that the two of them had gotten on a train in Clifton Forge that was bound for Washington, D.C. However, the trail ended there.

My class advisor, Miss Curry, came by the house on a regular basis to collect my schoolwork and she continued to assure me that everyone at school was totally convinced of my innocence, including the teachers and the principal. I was glad to have the assignments to work on at home as it helped to make the time pass faster. The days of waiting seemed to drag on and on. Endless days of waiting.

At breakfast on Wednesday morning, Dad suggested that the two of us go to the men's store and buy a new suit for me to wear to court. I reminded him that Tom had already told me to wear my red-letter sweater for the trial. The school sweater had two white stripes on the left sleeve and a big white "R" on the front. Words can't describe how much I loved that sweater.

"Along with the sweater, you should wear a clean white shirt without a tie on the day of the trial," my lawyer had advised me earlier. "I want the jury to see you as a clean cut high school student."

Dad nodded in agreement when I told him Tom's recommendation. The suit idea was quickly dropped and dad never mentioned it again.

Throughout that long week of waiting, I would count the hours each day until school was over so I could call Barb on the phone. The phone call with her was the highlight of each day. She was my strongest supporter and just hearing her voice seemed to renew my strength

Besides spending nearly an hour on the phone every day, Barb and I often took short walks together in the evening. Just being near her and holding her hand did a lot to lift my spirit. I felt like I was fighting in a war and sometimes actually felt like I had battle fatigue. I could only pray that my side would come out as the winner.

Sunday finally rolled around and once again I begged off from attending church with my parents. They understood and I hoped that

God understood too. I just couldn't handle the stares of all the curious people.

Max had been coming by every afternoon to spend some time with me and during his visits we would discuss what I had been reading in my Bible. Max told me that in his opinion, I was growing in the faith. I really didn't understand what that meant, but it sounded good to me.

That final Sunday evening as Barb and I strolled down the street near her house, she asked me if I had heard any more news about Jack and Anne. I brought her up to date on what Tom had related about the train they had taken to Washington.

"Towson, Maryland isn't too far from Washington," she remarked. "I remember that Anne told me once that she lived in Towson when she was a little girl. Maybe she still knows someone there. The two of them have to be somewhere. They couldn't have just disappeared, could they?"

There were still a lot of questions that didn't seem to have any answers. Maybe the answers would all come out at the trial.

Just as Barb was about to go inside her house, she turned and asked me if I was nervous about the upcoming trial.

Without hesitation I responded, "Sure I'm nervous. I'm nearly scared to death. Who wouldn't be?"

In my eyes, my life was on the line. I didn't talk to anyone about it, but sometimes I would be almost overwhelmed with fear. Cold, icy fingers of fear would grab me in a strangle hold and I would feel like I was going down for the final count.

Right there on her front porch, Barb suddenly wrapped both her arms around me and held me tight. "No, Jack! Don't be afraid. I just know everything is going to be all right. I know it! Believe me. It's going to be all right. Trust me!"

And at that moment, I did believe her and I felt the fear leave me.

CHAPTER 14

THE TRIAL

Finally it was the day of the trial. That Monday morning at nine-thirty sharp, Tom Ford came by the house to take me to the courthouse. Mom and Dad followed us over in their car. Tom had a big briefcase on the seat between us that he said was full of interviews he had conducted in the course of his investigation. He again told me not to worry because he had every confidence that the case would never go to the jury.

"I'm positive that Judge Hightower will dismiss the entire thing for lack of evidence on the State's part," he assured me. I only wished that I was as confident as Tom seemed to be. The fear had come back upon me.

We parked in the space reserved for attorneys and went into the courthouse. This morning we proceeded to the "real" courtroom, not the smaller hearing room where we had been previously.

I found myself entering a large room that could accommodate perhaps seventy-five to a hundred spectators. A sign outside of the door stated that seating was on a first come basis with fifteen seats reserved for the press and another ten for family.

I walked stiffly to the table that had been reserved for us, feeling every eye in the room looking in my direction. Tom motioned me to my chair, but before I could even sit down a court official marched in from a side door to announce the arrival of the judge.

"All rise!" he commanded in a loud voice. "The Shawnee County Court is now in session. The Honorable Judge Raymond J. Hightower, presiding." No sooner had he finished speaking when another door opened and Judge Hightower appeared wearing a black robe and took his seat on the bench. He looked very dignified and intimidating.

"Be seated," the official bellowed. With a shuffling of chairs, everyone took their seats and the courtroom was quiet.

My trial had officially begun.

Judge Hightower informed us that the morning session would probably be consumed with jury selection and that the afternoon would be taken up with opening remarks from the prosecuting and defense attorneys.

I thought that the jury selection was pretty interesting. The judge called twelve names from a list of prospective jurors and those chosen filed in from a side room and took a seat in the jury box. The State's attorney would then question each individual and either accept or challenge that person. From the first group, he rejected five prospective jurors. The first juror to be rejected had been one of my former Sunday school teachers and the next two to be turned down were neighbors. I guess in a small town like Redbank, it was hard to find anyone who didn't know me. But finally, Mr. Johnson settled on twelve people who met his qualifications as jurors. The five he rejected were told to leave the jury box.

Then Tom Ford was given his opportunity to question the jurors and he accepted the seven who remained in the box without even asking a question. Five more names were read from the list by the judge, and they entered the box and took the empty seats. It was a long slow process, but finally at eleven-thirty both attorneys seemed happy with the final jury.

By now I was pretty excited and ready to get the show on the road. I could hardly believe it when Judge Hightower announced that we were going to adjourn for lunch. After warning the jurors not to discuss the case during their lunch break, the judge departed from the room and the morning session came to an end.

At one-thirty everyone was back in their seats and the judge was back on the bench. The state's attorney, Mr. Aaron Johnson, was then called to address the jury and present his case. He talked for nearly two hours outlining everything that had taken place.

I had gone over all the details so many times with so many people, that I think I could have actually made the presentation myself. Mr. Johnson told about the untimely death of Dr. Adams and presented the coroner's report that stated that the cause of death was a gunshot wound to the head. He also commented to the jury that in his opinion Dr. Adams died instantly.

The presentation went on and on. The jury was informed about the weekly poker game at the Antler Club and that the doctor had left the club with winnings of over a thousand dollars at about eleven-fifty. Mr. Johnson was very precise in giving every detail to the jury. He left nothing out.

They were told how Dr. Adams arrived home at approximately 12:05 in the morning, parked his car in the garage but never came into the house. Everyone then heard about how the maid was sent to investigate and returned to tell Mrs. Adams that her husband had been shot and was dead.

The jury listened intently to every word. Mr. Johnson was an excellent speaker and his presentation was flawless. I even found myself leaning forward so that I wouldn't miss a word that he was saying.

"The police called me and I arrived at the Adams' home at about one-thirty," Mr. Johnson continued. "After visiting the crime scene and finding it just as the police had said, I interviewed Mrs. Adams. You can imagine that she was terribly upset over her husband's death."

At this time, Mr. Johnson moved closer to the jury box, pausing dramatically in his summary. He had the undivided attention of every juror, as well as everyone else in the courtroom.

"Then I spoke with Dr. Adam's sixteen year old daughter, Anne, and the interview was most interesting. She told me that she had been dating..." Looking down at his paper, he said, "I want to state exactly what her words were. Yes, here it is. His daughter told me that she had been dating Jack for some time and that they had become intimate. She informed me that she had recently missed her period and realized she was pregnant."

The jurors looked shocked. Although everyone knew about the murder, this was the first time that any of them had heard of these behind the scene details.

Mr. Johnson was getting just the reaction that he expected. Taking a deep breath, he continued on with further details about Anne's interview.

"When her father found out that Jack had gotten her pregnant, he was furious with Anne and with Jack. Anne told me that her father took her to his office in town, where she was given a shot. He then performed an abortion upon his daughter. After the procedure, Dr. Adams took the family to The Homestead in Hot Springs for a week where he kept Anne in complete seclusion."

Once again Mr. Johnson paused, giving the jurors time to digest the information they had just received.

"Finally, when Anne was home again and able to get to a phone, she called Jack and told him about everything that had happened. She further informed me that Jack went into an absolute rage and told her that he was going to fix her father."

At this point, my lawyer jumped to his feet and addressed the judge. "Your Honor, pardon me for interrupting, but may I have your permission to ask a question of the state's attorney at this time. I realize this is possibly out of order, but I believe it might serve to clarify a very important point and clear up some major confusion in this case."

The judge leaned forward on his bench. "This is highly unusual, Mr. Ford, but I will allow you one question," the judge replied.

Turning to address Mr. Johnson, Tom asked, "You have just stated that Anne Adams told you that Jack was the father of her unborn child. Here is my question: Exactly who is this Jack who is the father of the child? You keep talking about someone named Jack, but who is this Jack you're referring to over and over?"

Mr. Johnson hesitated a moment and then replied, "Well, Anne was obviously speaking of the defendant here, John White. Or Jack White as he is usually called by those who know him."

Tom quickly asked another question,. "Isn't there another Jack that Miss Adams had been spending quite a bit of time with in recent months? What about him? I ask you, what about the other Jack?"

It was obvious to everyone that Mr. Johnson was starting to feel uncomfortable with the questions that were being asked. Finally he spoke to Tom directly, "Are you referring to Jack Algood?"

"That's exactly who I'm referring to and you know it," Tom answered. "You are certainly aware that Jack Algood and Anne had been dating each other for much of the past year."

The judge pounded his gavel on the bench. "Gentlemen, gentlemen. Let's take minute to discuss this."

Tom Ford faced the judge and explained, "Your Honor, I believe that Miss Adams was referring to none other than Jack Algood when she spoke with Mr. Johnson the night of the murder. It is common knowledge that Anne and Jack Algood had been seeing each other for months. Mr. Johnson seems to have jumped to the conclusion that it was Jack White who was involved with Anne Adams instead of Jack Algood. This must be settled before we can continue with this trial."

"This is a very good point you have brought up, counselor," the judge stated. "I'm glad that you interrupted the proceedings to ask your question. Is there anyone who is able to clarify this point? Perhaps Miss Adams herself is available to testify."

Tom was still on his feet and responded quickly, "Unfortunately Miss Adams has been missing since the day after the murder, as has Jack Algood. However, her best friend, Barbara James, is right outside of the courtroom and she can give us a first hand account of the relationship between Jack Algood and Anne."

"Judge, this is highly irregular! I object!" shouted Mr. Johnson.

"Objection overruled!" the judge ordered. "Bailiff, call in Miss Barbara James."

The bailiff quickly left the courtroom and we could hear him through the open door saying, "Barbara James, please come with me. You're wanted in the courtroom."

Barb was looking a bit anxious as she made her way to the front of the room, but the judge spoke to her in a very reassuring voice. "Miss James, there are a few questions I would like to ask you. Don't be nervous now. If you just take the seat over there in the witness box, the bailiff will bring a Bible and swear you in."

Dressed in a plaid skirt, light blue cashmere sweater, bobby sox and saddle oxfords, I thought that Barb looked beautiful as she took the stand. I wondered if Tom Ford had told her what to wear. She looked like a typical American schoolgirl right out the pages of Seventeen magazine.

Barb was directed to place her left hand on the Bible and raise her right to take the oath. Her voice was a little shaky as she repeated the words given her by the bailiff, "I swear to tell the truth, the whole truth and nothing but the truth, so help me God."

The judge then looked directly at the two attorneys and said, "I am going to ask Miss James a few questions and both of you gentlemen will remain silent. Do you understand?"

Almost in unison the two men nodded their heads and replied, "Yes, your Honor."

The judge spoke gently to Barb, trying to get her to relax. "Do you mind if I call you Barb? Isn't that what everyone calls you?"

"Yes, sir. That would be fine. I'd like that," she answered quickly.

"I understand that you have been Anne Adams' best friend for quite some time. Is that correct?"

Barb nodded her head. I could tell that she was becoming much more comfortable now talking to the judge. She was even starting to smile a little.

"I suppose that as best friends you shared everything with each other, maybe even your closest secrets," the judge continued.

"Yes, sir," Barb said. "We never kept any secrets from each other. Anne and I talked together every day and we told each other everything."

"Did you know that Anne was pregnant?" Judge Hightower asked.

Barb thought for a minute before answering. "Well, I knew that she certainly thought that she was. She told me she had missed her period and didn't know how she was going to tell her parents that she was going to have a baby."

"And did Anne tell you who the father of her unborn child was?" the judge prompted.

Barb didn't hesitate a minute before answering. "Anne told me it was Jack. She said that Jack Algood had gotten her pregnant."

"Are you absolutely certain about this? Wasn't Anne dating Jack White at the time?" the judge fired back.

For a minute I thought that Barb was going to cry, but instead she sat up a little straighter and looked directly at the judge. I immediately knew she was going to tell the judge the truth about what had actually happened.

"No, sir," Barb replied. "Anne wasn't dating Jack White. She never dated Jack White. She was only pretending to date him. Jack White is my boyfriend and he always has been."

Barb was trying so hard to make the judge understand about our silly little cover up dating plan.

"Don't you understand, Judge? Anne was actually meeting secretly all the time with Jack Algood. Everything was just an act to keep her parents from knowing she was still seeing Jack Algood. I don't think that Jack White has ever spent more than ten minutes alone with Anne in his life."

The judge leaned back in his chair and asked, "So when Anne said that Jack was the father, she was actually talking about Jack Algood?"

"Yes, sir. I have told you the truth. Anne loved Jack Algood and he was the baby's father," Barb stated positively.

The judge smiled at Barb and dismissed her from the stand. "Thank you. I have no more questions. You may step down now."

"But, Judge, you haven't given me a chance to cross examine," shouted Aaron Johnson.

"Take it easy, Mr. Johnson," the judge stated firmly. "There will be no cross examination. This young lady has cleared up a very important point, one that you should have uncovered in your investigation. There has obviously been a question of mistaken identity here that has finally been exposed and brought to light."

The judge turned and faced the members of the jury. "On the basis of this testimony and other facts that were presented at the arraignment, I am dismissing all charges against the defendant. His record will be wiped clean and the case is closed. The jury is dismissed."

"Judge, I object!" shouted Mr. Johnson. But the judge had struck his gavel for the final time and already walked out of the courtroom.

Everything had happened so fast that I wasn't even sure exactly what had happened.

"What was that all about?" I asked Tom, feeling completely bewildered. "What am I supposed to do now?"

"Well, since all the charges against you have been dropped, I guess that the best thing for you to do right now is just go home and get on with your life."

We had a hard time getting out of the courtroom as there were so many people crowding around to congratulate us. The reporters were all running for the phones to call their stories in to their editors as quickly as possible. Tom finally grabbed me by the arm and escorted me out through a back door and away from all the commotion.

I didn't even get to see my parents until we arrived back at my house that was overflowing with friends and relatives. Everyone gathered around me when I walked in and it was pretty embarrassing to be the center of so much attention. Talk about a victory celebration!

Then my dad suddenly spied us from across the room and practically knocked folks over as he made his way toward us. I don't think he knew who to hug first, Tom or me. So he grabbed one of us in each arm and gave us each a big kiss on the cheek. I had never seen him so happy. Dad actually had tears in his eyes.

"Son, it's been an absolutely wonderful day," he exclaimed. "The truth has set you free."

Dad must have also heard that same still small voice that had spoken to my heart when I was in the jail and said, "You shall know the truth and the truth shall make you free."

The truth had been made known and now I was finally free.

CHAPTER 15

SUSPICIONS AROUSED

The day after the trial our phone wouldn't stop ringing. Mom finally took it off of the hook so that we could eat our breakfast in peace. Dad decided not to go into his office, declaring that this was a "family day" for the three of us.

About ten o'clock I phoned Barb. Her mother answered and seemed so happy to hear my voice that she hardly gave me a chance to say anything.

"Oh Jack, we are all so happy for you. I knew that Mr. Ford was going to call Barbara to the witness stand, but I had no idea that what she was going to say would be such a showstopper. Did you have any idea of what was going to happen?"

"No, ma'am. I was really surprised that the judge called her to the stand as quickly as he did. That's not the way they usually do it in the movies."

I was glad to talk to Mrs. James, but I really wanted to spend some time with Barb on the phone. Finally I was able to break in and asked, "Could I please talk to Barb for a few minutes?"

Mrs. James laughed and reminded me that it was Tuesday morning. "Jack, have you forgotten? This is a school day and Barbara is at school right now."

I felt really foolish. "I'm sorry," I responded. "Things have been so crazy lately that I had totally forgotten that everyone was still going to school. My teachers have been sending my assignments home for me, so that's where I've been doing all of my studying. Could you please have Barb call me as soon as she gets home?"

"Of course," Mrs. James replied. "Incidentally, have you seen today's paper? Your picture is on the front page and on page two there is a photo of Barbara. The trial has really put Redbank in the news."

Not only had I forgotten about school, but I had also forgotten about the publicity that the trial had generated. It was foolish to think that all the gossip and notoriety was going to die down immediately.

"I haven't seen the paper yet, but I'll get hold of one soon," I informed Mrs. James. "I'll be so glad when this whole thing is over and done with." I paused before adding, "Please don't forget to have Barb call me."

"Don't worry, I won't," Mrs. James told me. "Have a good day."

As I hung up the phone, I knew it was going to be a good day because I was free. The trial was over and I believed that my life would soon be back to normal."

Our daily paper, The Staunton News, had a big picture of me on the front page with a headline that read: "Redbank Boy Exonerated In Surprise Trial Ending." And there on page two was the photo of Barb that her mother had mentioned. "Star Witness Gives Key Testimony," the headline under Barb's picture stated in large letters. The newspaper had devoted almost two full pages to the trial along with a recap of the murder. Where did those reporters find so much to write about?

Looking the various stories in the paper, I really felt like I was reading about someone else. Had all of this happened to me? I looked at the picture again to confirm that it was really me. I wondered if the day would ever come when this would all be forgotten and I would be just plain old Jack White again.

Later that day when I contacted the school to ask about returning, I was informed that I could report for class the following day. I was actually excited about getting back to my studies. "It will sure be great to get back onto a regular routine," I thought, realizing that it had been over two weeks since I had been to school.

But school was anything but routine. I hadn't even set foot on school property before kids were stopping me and asking all sorts of questions:

Did you like jail? (You've got to be kidding!) Were you scared? (Sure I was scared. You would have been too.) Did they give you the third degree with the lights and all?(No bright lights or anything like that. We sat in a room at a table. They asked me questions and I gave them answers.) Who do you think killed old man Adams? (I had an idea who it was, but I wasn't about to tell them.)

On and on the questions continued until the first class bell finally rang. In every class I attended that day, the teacher gave me a pleasant greeting and told me how glad everyone was to have me back. I may have been viewed as somewhat of a celebrity, but I had no special privileges and no less homework than anyone else. I was actually starting to feel like Jack White again.

It was about two weeks before things really settled down. The questions at school stopped and I went back to work at Mr. James' hardware store after school and on Saturdays. Barb and I continued to see each other and often talked on the phone. However, our relationship wasn't as comfortable as it had been previously. Everything that had happened with Anne and Jack hung over us like a dark cloud and the two of them were never far from our thoughts.

I had my suspicions about who had killed Dr. Adams, but the only people I voiced them with were Barb and my attorney, Tom Ford. I had shared with both of them at various times how I strongly suspected that Jack Algood was the one who was responsible for the death of Dr. Adams and that he was the one the police should be seeking to arrest.

I knew for a fact that Jack had been really upset over what Dr. Adams had done to end Anne's pregnancy. And I also knew from personal experience that Jack had a real problem controlling his anger and I had often seen him lose his cool. I couldn't deny the evidence that pointed to him.

And then there was the gun. When Jack has noticed the burn on my hand several months ago, I had told him about the pistol. I was now positive that I had also mentioned to him about hiding the gun in the old lunch box in the garage. Then when Jack and Anne turned up missing, I felt certain that not only Jack was involved in the crime, but also Anne.

Barb agreed with my suspicions, but Tom was not nearly as convinced as we were. However, he said that he would speak with the police about the matter. A few days later, I heard that the state police had issued a bulletin asking for information about John. R. Algood, also known as Jack Algood. The notice also stated that he might be accompanied by Anne Adams aged sixteen and that they had last been seen on a C&O train bound for Washington, D.C. Jack's picture was printed on the bulletin.

Christmas and New Year's came and went, almost lost in the drama of recent events. There was still no response from the bulletin that had been distributed. I found myself wondering if the search for Jack and Anne was still continuing or if anyone still even remembered that they were missing.

The thought of Jack, my best friend, having actually committed a murder, was almost more than I could handle. In some ways I felt responsible because I had helped Jack and Anne to continue their relationship. I wondered what I could have done to prevent the whole thing from happening, but it was too late to change things now.

But I hadn't forgotten Jack and Anne and every night when I went to bed, I would say a prayer asking God to bring them back home.

Winter gave way to spring and as graduation approached there was still no word on either of them When the class of '51 crossed the platform in May and received their diplomas, my classmates and I were officially recognized as seniors. As the Class of 1952, we were ready to begin our final year at Redbank High School.

CHAPTER 16

TURKEY BOWL

Football practice started in the middle of August, just as it had for the past three years. But this year something was different. My best buddy wasn't playing at halfback. I was still a fixture at right end, but it just didn't seem the same not to be blocking downfield to clear the way for Jack Algood. The guy now running at Jack's old position was only a sophomore, but I had to admit that he was a fast and shifty runner.

The Red Raiders started the season off with a big win and we never looked back. We won every game, usually by big margins. There was talk of a challenge for a Turkey Bowl game with the one other undefeated team in the state, Lane High School of Charlottesville. Lane was a much larger school than Redbank High. Two of their juniors had placed on the All-State team the previous year, their quarterback and one running back. I read where those players were receiving All-Star ratings again this year.

After our final game, which we had won 42 to 0, our coach called the team together with some big news. The coach from Lane High had just called him and challenged us to a game on Thanksgiving Day. The match would settle the big question of which team was the best in the state of Virginia.

Would we accept the challenge? Without hesitation the unanimous vote of the entire squad was, "Yes! We can beat them!"

So it was definitely game on! After much dickering between the coaches and principals of the two schools, it was finally decided that the championship game would be played in Harrisonburg, Virginia in the stadium of James Madison College. It was a neutral site and the Dukes had finished their season the middle of November.

The whole county was excited over the news. It was hard to imagine that a small school from Shawnee County would be playing against a school the size of Lane High. The Ruritan Club even took up an offering and bought our entire team new molded plastic helmets to replace the old leather style we were currently wearing. The new helmets were white with a red stripe down the middle. The word "Raiders" was printed on both sides and they gave us a really classy look.

Not to be outdone, the Antler Club got into the act and donated brand new uniforms for everyone. They were made of nylon, the shiny stretch kind, with red pants and white jerseys. The red pants had a white stripe running down the outside of each leg and the white jerseys had "Raiders" written in red letters with three red stripes on each sleeve.

One afternoon we were allowed to put the uniforms on to have a team picture taken and we were an impressive looking group. With the new uniforms and helmets, we certainly looked like a winning team. Only time would tell if we would walk away from the Turkey Bowl as the victors.

Our Red Raiders' team was really elated about the prospect of playing in a real stadium before a huge crowd from all over northwestern Virginia. The Black Knights were reported to be one of the largest and most powerful high school teams in the entire state. The newspapers had already predicted Lane High as the winners of the big game by a margin of over twenty points, but that just served to fire us up even more. We were going to show everyone that the Red Raiders was a team to be reckoned with when we faced the Black Knights.

The big day finally arrived and the trip to Harrisonburg was a real blast. The team bus was followed by a long line of supporters' cars that were all decked out with red and white streamers. Everyone in the cars would blow their horns as we passed through each town on our journey northward.

However, on the bus the attitude was much more somber. The coach had done his best to keep our minds strictly on the game that awaited us. He had even arranged for the cheerleaders to ride in cars with some of the folks who were following in our caravan. He wanted our minds on the game and not on the girls.

I could hardly wait for the opening kickoff that we had elected to receive. Taking the ball at the fifteen-yard line, we pushed it steadily down field and were able to score on our first drive. The Black Knights, in their solid black uniforms with orange trim, came right back at us and drove the ball back down the field and in for a score. That's the way it went for the entire first half, which ended with Lane High School leading by seven points with a score of 28 to 21.

The second half of the game continued very much like the first two quarters. One team would score and then the other. The game see-sawed back and forth. The victory was going to take place only after a hard fought battle. With just two minutes to go in the final quarter, Lane scored on a long pass to bring the score to 34 to 28. They had missed an extra point along the way.

We had one last chance and only two minutes to pull off the biggest win in school history. Maybe even in state history. The kickoff came to the sophomore who had taken Jack Algood's place, and he brought the ball out to the thirty-five yard line. Unfortunately, in the next three plays, we only gained four yards.

It was now fourth down with six yards to go and only thirty seconds left on the clock. As the tension mounted, the coach called for a time out. He was sending in a final play for us. It was called the "Red Raider Special - Right." We had practiced that play a hundred times, but had never run it in a game all season. The play called for me to take six steps downfield directly toward their defensive back. I was then to make a sharp cut to the right and in the process was to intentionally lose my footing and fall. This ploy should cause the opposing defender to take his eyes off of me momentarily and to follow the faint of our quarterback who was looking to the left. At that moment, the pass would be tossed to me just as I regained my feet. It was a long shot, but if it worked we had a chance to win the big game.

Of course, the question was, would it work? Would their defensive back be drawn away? We had nothing to lose and everything to gain. In the next thirty seconds we would find out if the "Red Raider Special" was special enough to give us the victory.

The quarterback called the signals: "Ready! Set! Sixty-two! Thirty-nine. Hut! Hut! Hut!"

The ball was snapped and the quarterback retreated. I ran my route and slipped according to the plan. Lane High's defensive back moved to his right, away from me, and suddenly the pass was in the air heading right toward my uplifted arms. I was wide open to receive it.

Sixty-one yards of open field stretched out before me. The umpire ran along with me step for step. As I crossed the goal line, he lifted his hands to the heavens. I had made the touchdown and the game was tied with a score of 34 to 34. The crowd cheered. Victory was in sight!

We lined up for the point after attempt and the stadium was hushed as the ball was snapped and placed for the extra point try. Thump! The ball was in the air. Again the referee's hands reached skyward. The point was good. The Red Raiders were ahead by 35 to 34 with only two seconds remaining on the clock.

Amid the wild and exuberant shouts from our joyful fans, the ball was placed at the forty-yard line in readiness for the kick off. The long kick brought the ball nearly to the goal line where the Black Knight receiver fumbled. As he fell on the ball at the two-yard line, the whistle blew. The game was over! The Red Raiders had accomplished the impossible! We were the champs. We had proven that we were the BEST!

It was amazing! The Red Raiders of little Redbank High School had not only completed the season undefeated, but had beaten one of the strongest teams in Virginia. Talk about elation! I can't even describe the emotion that our team was feeling at that time. We were ecstatic! We were on a high unlike any high that kids our age had ever experienced! We were the champions! We were victorious! We were carried off of the field as conquering heroes!

If I had thought that the drive over to Harrisonburg that morning had been loud with all the horns blowing, it was nothing compared to the noise generated on the ride back home that night. And when we arrived in Redbank, we found Main Street lined with cheering fans who formed a parade and led our caravan over to the high school football field.

The entire town was waiting there to welcome us back and to celebrate our great victory. There was singing and dancing and shouting and cheering. I had never seen anything like it.

It was like everyone was there to take part in the festivities that night. Even the mayor and the chief of police attended. School children had come out carrying little red and white flags and brightly colored balloons. I noticed that the little old ladies from the church sewing circle were there to take part in this momentous occasion.

As the evening wore on, things did get a little rowdy. Some folks built a bonfire and nearly burned down the bleachers. But it only added to the excitement when the fire department showed up on the scene. It was a definitely a night to remember.

What a great way to end my high school football career!

CHAPTER 17

FUTURE PLANS

Christmas of 1951 came and went with the usual celebration. The town put up colored lights on Main Street and all the businesses decorated their windows with snowmen and Christmas trees.

Someone donated new signs that had been erected at the entrances into town that read, "Redbank, Home of the Undefeated Red Raiders." It was a nice touch but I was concerned that civic pride might have been carried too far.

Shortly after Christmas our class began to make plans for the junior-senior prom. Since there were never enough seniors to put on their own class prom, Redbank High School had always held a combined prom. The junior class did the decorating and the seniors did the celebrating. The prom was always held the third week of May with graduation taking place a week later, just a day or two before school closed for the summer.

It was toward the end of March when Barb gave me the news that she had applied to the University of Kentucky and been accepted. She was going to be leaving for school the third week of August. I really hadn't given too much thought to college and certainly had never considered Kentucky. That was way too far from home. All I really knew about the school was that their nickname was "The Wildcats" and that their colors were blue and white.

The night Barb told me about her acceptance, I almost cried. We had been through so much the past year that it had never occurred to me that we would ever be separated. Barb assured me that we would write to one another and that she would be home for every holiday as well as in the summer.

Then she asked me the big question, "Where are you going to college?"

I had no idea of how to answer her. Several schools had contacted me asking if I would consider trying out for their football teams. One inquiry was from Virginia Military Institute in Lexington. I was pretty sure that my attorney, Tom Ford, had a hand in getting that letter sent to me since I knew he had graduated from VMI. The other invitation had come from a college in West Virginia called Shepherd State College. I had never even heard of that school before.

But Barb's question about college really made me think. I knew it cost a lot of money to go to college, but without some education beyond high school, I wondered what sort of job would be open for me. For the first time I really began to think about my future.

It was about this same time that an army recruiter came by our school to talk with the senior boys. He gave an excellent presentation and informed us that the Army offered all kinds of programs that taught various skills that could be used later in civilian life. The recruiter was very truthful and advised us that we would have to sign up for a three-year enlistment to even be considered for admission to one of their special training programs.

The things this army representative was saying really caught my attention, especially when he remarked that army service would entitle a recruit to the benefits of the GI Bill. The government would actually pay for a college education when army service was completed.

We were also informed that a special test was going to be offered in two weeks at the recruiting office in Staunton, the results of which would determine if application could be made for one of the special schools At the end the recruiter's talk, we were given several pamphlets outlining a number of programs available to qualifying enlistees.

This opportunity for training almost seemed like an answer to prayer. However, later that afternoon I realized that the recruiter hadn't mentioned one word about the Korean War that was currently being waged. Nor had he advised us that those who didn't qualify for an army school would go directly into the infantry after basic training and probably be sent off to Korea. There were definite drawbacks, but at the time they didn't seem very important to me. I was pretty fired up about everything I had heard.

The night after the recruiter's visit to the school, I sat down with Dad and talked about what I should do when I graduated in May. I knew that we didn't have a lot of money for college and I wasn't really sure I wanted to continue playing football. I had to admit that the information about the GI Bill sounded good, but I certainly didn't relish the thought of ending up in Korea if I didn't succeed in their special program.

Dad really seemed to enjoy our discussion together and suggested that we both pray about the situation. That sounded good to me and I had a long talk with the Lord that night. Later the thought came to me that I would be saving my folks a lot of money if I didn't go to college, money that they could be putting away for when Dad retired.

The more I thought about going into the Army, the better the idea seemed. Three years in the Army could give me valuable experience that I could use in a civilian job. A three-year enlistment in the Army certainly seemed to be a reasonable alternative to taking a low paying job locally or going off to college for four years right now. I also realized that if I went to college and didn't keep my grades up, the draft was a certainty. And it was common knowledge that anyone who was drafted would end up in the infantry and then be shipped off to Korea. I sure didn't want that to happen to me.

The next day my dad and I talked again and it was decided that I would go to Staunton and take the test that the Army was offering.

Then I would wait to see the results of the examination and based on them would make a final decision about whether or not to enlist.

So about ten days later, Dad loaned me his car and I made the trip to Staunton. When I arrived at the recruiting station I found out that I was to take a whole battery of tests. The intensive examination was geared to not only test basic knowledge on a variety of subjects, but also to determine a person's aptitude in various skills.

I was confident and relaxed as I took the exam and felt that I had done pretty well. When I was finished and ready to head back home, the sergeant in charge said that I would be receiving a letter concerning the results within the next ten days.

But it took only six days for the official letter to arrive and I learned that I had scored very well on the entire battery of tests. Based on the results, I had qualified for enlistment into a super secret army group called the Army Security Agency. The letter informed me that if I enlisted immediately upon graduation from high school, I would have only eight weeks of basic training instead of the usual sixteen required for those going into the infantry. Then when I completed basic, I would be sent to a base in Massachusetts where I would begin my specialized training.

To say I was excited was an understatement. There was an acceptance form that my parents and I were required to sign and return to the Army Office of Recruitment. My hand was shaking a little as I wrote my name. It was a big decision for a seventeen year old to be making.

Several days passed before I received a reply from the army office. Mom was waiting at the door when I came home from school with the letter in her hand. I think she was as anxious as I was to see what it said.

To our surprise, the letter advised me that there was a problem with my enlistment. It seemed that there was already someone in the United States Army by the name of John Charles White and his date of birth was the same as mine. I was informed that the soldier's place of birth was recorded as Redbank, Virginia and that his parents had the same exact names as my parents. They wrote that before I could be accepted into the Army, there would need to be some clarification of the duplicate information.

I was shocked to say the least and so was my mother. We both stood there speechless as we read the letter. Dad was also flabbergasted when we phoned him and related the contents of the letter. Certainly to our knowledge there was not another John Charles White anywhere, much less in Redbank. There obviously would have to be an investigation.

Who else but Tom Ford, our attorney, could assist us with this matter? Tom had experience with the Army and probably still had contact with a few friends in high places who could help him straighten out this crazy mixed-up situation. Dad immediately called Tom who came right over to read the letter for himself. He agreed that there had to be some logical explanation. Once again we were obviously facing a question of mistaken identity.

Several days went by with no word from Tom. I read the letter over and over trying to figure out how this could have possibly happened. And then information began to come from all directions. Tom had sent out queries to the Army and to a friend or two in the Pentagon. He had also visited the county clerk's office to check the official birth records. Slowly the truth began to emerge.

At the county clerk's office, Tom learned that a birth certificate had been issued to someone claiming to be John Charles White back in mid-August. A young man had come in asking for a copy of his birth certificate and had given his date of birth as May 30, 1934. He had also provided the names of my parents when asked. The girl who had handled the matter was new in the office, but she remembered that the person making the request had blonde hair and blue eyes and was about the right age. Apparently he had told her that he needed the birth certificate for something official at school.

Tom then asked us if anyone we knew matched that description. I immediately thought of Jack Algood. He certainly knew my birthday and my parents' names. Plus Jack had blonde hair and blue eyes. Could he have stolen my identification in order to enlist in the army?

Further investigation led Tom to discover that a copy of my birth certificate had been used a short time later to obtain a West Virginia driver's license. He also learned that the person who enlisted in the Army under my name had used a West Virginia driver's license as well as a Virginia birth certificate as proof of identification.

Digging deeper into the mystery, Tom was led to the West Virginia State Police Station in Franklin, which is the county seat of Pendleton County. Franklin is located just a few miles up Route 220 from Redbank, just across the West Virginia state line. The people working there remembered a person using my name who had come in, shown a birth certificate and taken the driving test. He had given an address in Harper, West Virginia, a small town just south of Franklin. The license that was issued listed the individual as five feet ten inches tall and weighing one hundred and eighty pounds with blonde hair and blue eyes. The description fit Jack Algood exactly.

That cinched it! Jack Algood had not only stolen my identity but he had also enlisted in the Army using my name. It didn't seem possible that someone I had always considered to be my best friend would do something like that. But then again, Jack had also stolen my gun from the garage and made it look like I had killed Dr. Adams. My best friend was apparently my worst enemy. I wondered where Jack was now.

From army records, Tom discovered that Jack Algood, also known as Private John C. White, had enlisted at Fort Meade, Maryland on December 30, 1951. Jack had been sent to Camp Campbell in Kentucky for his basic training. After completing four weeks of training, he was given a twenty-four hour pass on February 3rd and granted permission to go into Clarksville, Tennessee for the night. However, Jack failed to return to the base and the following evening had been found by the military police drunk in an alley.

It was a sad story. Jack was returned to Camp Campbell and confined to the stockade where he completed his basic training under armed guard. On March 14, 1952, he was sent to Korea and assigned to an infantry battalion. Within two days of his arrival in Korea, Jack assaulted a sergeant, was arrested and sent to Japan to face a court martial. While under guard on a train in route to the army base, he managed to escape. Jack was found dead outside of a bar on the outskirts of Tokyo several days later. He was buried in a grave in Japan on March 27th.

When all of this was brought to the light, Jack's army records were amended and any reference to my name was removed. There was once again only one John Charles White from Redbank, Virginia.

The mystery of Jack Algood was solved, but one other mystery remained. What had happened to Anne Adams?

That mystery was solved on the first of May when Anne got off of a bus in downtown Redbank and walked to her home on Lee Street. Very few people in town would have even recognized her that day because she had changed so completely. Anne had lost a great deal of weight and her beautiful black hair had been dyed red. Her eyes were sunken back into her head and there were dark circles under them. It was hard to believe that this was the same person who had left Redbank less than two years before.

I can only imagine the shock Anne had when she arrived home and saw the change that had taken place in her mother. After her husband's death and Anne's departure, Mrs. Adams had gone on a drinking binge and it had taken some time for her to sober up again. Missie Williams, her faithful maid, continued to work for Mrs. Adams, taking care of the house and doing the cooking.

Anne's mother had just gotten back on her feet again when Dr. Adams' will went to probate. At the reading of the will, three women showed up at the lawyer's office, each claiming that the doctor had been her husband. Two of them turned out to be seeking marital status based on common-law relationships. Both of these claims were found to be invalid and dismissed.

The third woman, who currently lived on Dr. Adams' farm in Monterey, was the mother of a twelve-year-old son. The boy's birth certificate had been issued at John Hopkins Hospital in Baltimore and listed the father's name as Andrew Anderson Adams. The name of the child? Andrew Anderson Adams, Jr. His mother also produced a marriage certificate that had been issued in Elkton, Maryland, a well-known "quickie-marriage" town, just seven months prior to her son's birth.

It turned out that Dr. Adams was a bigamist! He had been living a double life. Perhaps he had even been living a quadruple life. Yet the citizens of Redbank had always considered Dr. Adams to be a very respectable, though eccentric, gentleman. I guess life is full of surprises.

In the end, the judge who was overseeing the probate awarded the second Mrs. Adams the farm in Monterey, Virginia plus ten thousand dollars in cash. He also required that a trust fund in the sum of fifty thousand dollars be set up for Dr. Adam's son.

Anne's mother? She inherited the house on Lee Street and the remainder of Dr. Adams' financial wealth. In the will it was stated that Anne was to receive what remained of the doctor's estate upon the death of Mrs. Adams.

That day in May, Anne arrived home to a much different situation than she expected to find. So many things had changed. She probably wished that she had never gotten off the bus.

CHAPTER 18

ANNE'S RETURN

It was several days after Anne's return to Redbank before either Barb or I heard that she was back. Actually Barb was the first to get the word. She was just coming out of her father's store when who should she see walking down the street lugging a large bag of groceries but Missie Williams, the Adams' maid.

"Missie," Barb called out. "I haven't seen you for so long. How are you? Has there been any news of Anne?"

"Hi there, Miss James," Missie replied. "Nice to see you. Haven't you heard? Miss Anne done come home three nights ago. She was certainly a sight for sore eyes."

Missie paused and shifted her groceries to the other arm. "But Miss Anne come home looking really bad. She done lost probably thirty pounds while she was away and you should see her hair all dyed red. And she was so dirty. I don't think she had a bath in days."

Barb opened her mouth and was about to ask something, but there was no stopping Missie. She had started the story and she was going to finish telling it.

"Mrs. Adams was pretty drunk as usual at the time Miss Anne got home, but she done sobered up real quick when she realized who Anne was. Miss Barb, you gotta come by soon and see your friend."

With these final words, Missie turned away, "Sorry I can't talk long with you, but this bag is awful heavy and I gotta get on home. Bye now, Miss Barb." Having said her piece, Missie headed off down the street, having no idea of the effect her words had upon Barb.

Barb hurried back into the store and found me down in the basement getting some merchandise to restock the shelves. "Jack you're never going to believe what I just heard. Anne is home!"

"You must be kidding!" I responded. "Who told you that?"

"I just ran into Mrs. Adams' maid, Missie. She had been out shopping and I saw her as I was on my way home. She told me all about everything. I'm going upstairs to Dad's office and call Anne right now.'

As Barb started up the stairs, she said, "Come on, Jack. You can listen in on the extension."

"Just a minute," I replied. "Let me get these things on the shelves and I'll be right with you. Go ahead and make the call."

A thousand thoughts raced through my mind. Where had Anne been? Did she know about Jack? Had the police found her and brought her home?

As I picked up the extension, I heard Barb asking, "Where did you say you've been all this time?"

And then I heard Anne's familiar voice. "Baltimore. I've been in Baltimore," Anne answered. "Jack and I took the train from Clifton Forge to Washington when we left and then caught a bus to Baltimore. Jack told me that he was sure we could find a place to stay and that he had heard there were plenty of jobs available."

"We thought that you were going to get married," Barb commented.

"I thought so too," Anne said in reply. "But instead Jack forced me to work at a place on East Baltimore Street. Have you ever heard of that street?"

When Barb didn't answer right away, Anne continued. "No, of course you haven't. The street is full of bars and strip clubs and I think that the mob actually runs everything. Blaze Starr, the stripper, has a club there and I worked just down the block from her place."

I'm not sure that Barb knew quite how to respond to Anne's comment, but finally she came out and asked, "What did you do there in Baltimore?"

There was silence before Anne answered. "You really don't want to know and I don't want to tell you. That's all behind me now and I'm never going back to Baltimore."

Again there was a moment of silence before Anne continued. "I know that I should have stayed here to be with mother after Daddy died, but Jack insisted that we had to get out of town. He said that the police were going to be looking for him and that we had to leave Redbank. I really didn't see how we could afford to leave, but then Jack pulled a big wad of bills out of his pocket and told me that we didn't have to worry about money. He had more than enough."

Anne's voice cracked and I thought for a minute that she was going to cry. But she took a deep breath and finished her story.

"Jack didn't even give me time to get any clothes together. He just rushed me out of the house and told me to get into his dad's car. We drove to the train station in Clifton Forge and left the car there."

I could tell that Anne didn't want to talk about their escape. She quickly changed the subject and said, "Oh, Barb. I'm so glad to be home. I've been so lonely."

Barb was sympathetic. "It sounds like you've really been through it these past months. When are we going to get together?" Barb asked.

"You won't like what you see," Anne stated. "I look really different. Give me a few days to get my act together and I'll give you a call when I'm ready to sit down for a long talk." There was another pause before Anne spoke again. "I've got to hang up now. I think I hear my mother coming."

With that Anne hung up the phone and Barb and I were left to ponder everything that we had just heard about Anne's time in Baltimore.

The few days she spoke of turned into more than a week. Anne finally called Barb on Friday and said that she was ready to see us. "Bring Jack along," she suggested. "Is he still driving old Lizzy?"

Barb laughed and said that I could probably borrow my dad's car for the Friday when we got together.

We picked Anne up at seven-thirty and decided to just go park somewhere to spend some private time together. If we had gone to one of the usual hangouts like the Sweet Shop, we probably would have run into a lot of people that we knew and that was the last thing that Anne needed right now. So we found a quiet place and just pulled in and parked the car. Barb and I were in the front seat with Anne in the back, so we turned around to talk with each other.

I hardly recognized Anne. The cute little brunette I had known since grade school certainly was not the person in the back seat. Before she left town, Anne had short hair and bangs. Now her hair was long and dyed red. Her complexion had a pallid look to it, more grey than pink, and her lipstick was bright red and applied way too thickly. Is this really Anne, I wondered.

I was shocked by Anne's appearance, but even more so by what she told us that night in the car about her experience after she left Redbank.

It seems that when the two of them had arrived in Baltimore, Jack took her directly to East Baltimore Street, an area commonly referred to as "The Block." Someone had given Jack an address for a place called "The Show Girl," a nightclub of sorts, and told him they were always looking for pretty young girls to work there. Anne told us that after a brief interview with the manager, they had both been offered a job. Jack was going to be what was called a bouncer.

"Were you a waitress?" Barb asked innocently.

Anne hesitated before answering. "Well, some of the time I just sat and talked with the customers while they drank whiskey and watched the show. But other times I had to go upstairs and entertain men. That was horrible, but Jack threatened to beat me up if I didn't do it. I was afraid of him. It was like Jack had gone absolutely crazy."

"Why didn't you leave?" Barb asked.

"I didn't know where to go. Jack never gave me any money and hardly ever let me out of his sight. He had started hanging around with some really tough guys who carried guns in their waistbands. You can't possibly imagine what it was like. I was terrified."

Anne choked up as she tried to describe her experience.

"Then about a week before Christmas, Jack got into some real trouble with his new friends. Apparently he was carrying a large amount of money for them from one club to another and decided to keep some of it for himself. They came and tore our room apart looking for Jack and the money. But he had gone into hiding somewhere. He didn't even come back to spend Christmas with me."

But Anne wasn't finished with the story yet. "I thought that I'd never see Jack again, but three days after Christmas, I think it was December 28th, Jack slipped into the room about four o'clock in the morning. He gave me a hundred dollars, took some papers he had hidden in one of the drawers and said he was leaving town. I haven't seen him since."

"Gosh, Anne. I really don't know what to say," I stammered. "Didn't you know that the police were looking for the two of you?"

"I thought they might be. That's why I never came back, I was afraid." Anne responded. "About a month after we arrived in Baltimore Jack told me all about the night my father was killed. He said that he was so angry with Dad when he heard about the abortion that he couldn't control himself. He told me about everything that had happened."

Turning to address me, Anne said, "Jack even told me about how he went over to your house that awful night and took the gun he knew you had hidden in the lunch box. And then he told me how he waited in our garage for my father to come home. He confessed everything to me. Jack killed my father! He actually killed my father!"

Anne was weeping now and there were also tears running down Barb's face. I have to admit that my eyes were watering too.

"You need to talk with the police and tell them everything you've shared with us, Anne. Would you be willing to do that?" I asked. "I can arrange things with a great attorney I know. The police need to hear this so they can wrap up the case of your father's murder."

"Do you really think I should tell them?" Anne questioned.

"Yes, Anne. You definitely should," I replied firmly.

Anne paused before finally asking, "What will happen to me?"

"You will be seen as an innocent victim. I know in my heart that everything is going to be all right. All you have to do is tell the truth," I answered. "Just tell them the truth." The truth had set me free and I knew that it would set Anne free too.

"I wonder where Jack is now and what he's doing?" Anne murmured.

I realized that no one had told Anne what we had found out about Jack just a short time before. She really needed to know where Jack had gone and what he had done after leaving her in Baltimore. It wasn't an easy story to tell but she needed to know the truth and about Jack's death in Japan.

As I finished Anne said, "I'm really not surprised to hear that his life ended that way. I had a feeling that I would never see Jack alive again. It's all so sad, so very sad."

The three of us were quiet on the ride back to Anne's house. There really didn't seem to be anything else to say. The time had come to forget the things that were past and look forward with hope.

As Anne got out of the car, I assured her that I would contact Tom Ford the next day. Then I did something that I had never done before. I took her hand in mine and prayed for her asking God to be with her and give her peace.

CHAPTER 19

GRADUATION

The next day I phoned Tom Ford to tell him that Anne was back home. I informed him that Jack had taken her to Baltimore and forced her to work in a real sleazy place on East Baltimore Street. Tom had heard about the infamous "Block" and was shocked to learn that Anne had been serving in a club there. It seemed so out of character for a nice girl from Redbank. Tom said that he would contact the state police about Anne being back in town and they would get in touch with her.

I then asked Tom if anyone had ever notified Mrs. Algood about Jack's death in Japan. I thought it was possible that the Army had contacted her once Jack had been positively identified. Mrs. Algood's husband had passed away several months ago and she was living alone as a widow. What a crushing blow it was going to be to her to learn that her only son was also dead. Not only that, but that he had died a dishonorable death.

"I don't believe that anyone has told her yet," Tom replied. "Maybe I should get in touch with Reverend Max MacCormick and the two of us can go by her house together to break the news. I expect she is going to take this very hard. I know that I would certainly be mortified if a son of mine had died under such circumstances."

I asked Tom to let me know after he had visited her. "I know my mother will want to go by to see her too. Mom knows how to handle situations like this," I assured him. "And I want to thank you again for helping to get this whole business straightened out."

That evening when I was talking with Barb during our usual phone call, she told me that she had been by to see Anne again. "Anne still looks really bad," Barb told me, "but I actually think that her mom looks even worse."

Apparently Anne's mother stayed drunk most of the time and wasn't taking care of herself at all. Barb said that she had arrived at Anne's house before eleven o'clock and Anne's mother was already pouring herself a drink. The maid seemed to be in charge of running the house.

There had been so much bad news lately that I wanted to talk with Barb about something good for a change, so I brought up the subject of the upcoming prom. I wondered if she still wanted to go with me.

"Have you thought any more about the prom?" I asked.

Barb sounded happy when she replied. "I think about it all the time. I want to go and I want to go with you. Is your invitation still open?"

Those were just the words that I wanted to hear. "It sure is and there's not another girl anywhere that I would rather take to the prom," I responded. "We're going to have a great time. It's going to be terrific!"

Then Barb asked me what I had heard from the Army. I told her about the letter I had recently received informing me that I should report to the recruiting station in Staunton on June the third. "My understanding is that from there I will be transported to Arlington, Virginia where I'll be sworn in before continuing on to Fort Meade, Maryland for initial processing," I informed her

"June the third," Barb repeated. "That's not very far off, is it? I really thought that I would be at college before you went into the Army.

What is it going to be like to be apart like this? We've been so close the past couple of years. Oh Jack, I'm going to miss you so much."

I grew sad even thinking of being separated from Barb. "I guess we'll just have to get used to it. We can still see each other over your school holidays. I think I can probably get leave at the same time you'll be at home."

But even as I spoke those words, I knew it would never be the same again. I was lying to myself when I said that nothing was going to change.

Barb sighed deeply. "I'm sure that both of us will adjust in time, but I'm not going to think about it now," she stated.

"Me neither!" I replied. "I'll see you at school tomorrow."

I sat by the phone for a long time just thinking about the future, wondering what it would hold. Would Barb and I continue to have a relationship after graduation? Would I be shipped off to some foreign country and never see her again? Only time would tell.

When I got home from school the next afternoon there was a message from Tom asking me to return his call. I was anxious to hear what he had to say and phoned him back almost immediately.

He said that he had talked with the state police and they were going to be stopping by Anne's house to interview her. Tom also informed me that he and "Rev. Max" (as he called him), had visited with Mrs. Algood. It had not been an easy visit and Tom said he was very grateful that he hadn't gone alone. Max had been the one to break the news to Mrs. Algood and had handled it beautifully. I advised Tom that I was sure that my mother would soon be going over to spend time with Mrs. Algood and to see what she could do to help her deal with her grief.

Four days before the prom, something very interesting happened Three guys from the sophomore class stopped me in the hall after school with a question. "Would you be willing to sell Lizzy to us?"

I hadn't even thought about Lizzy for several weeks. With my arrest, the trial and my enlistment in the Army, I had completely lost interest in the old car. I hadn't taken her out for a spin in months. There were so many other things in my life that were more important than a Model A Ford.

"I would certainly be willing to sell her to you, but I'll have to check with the others first to see how they feel about it. I could let you know in a couple of days. How much would you be willing to pay for the car?' I asked.

I could tell that they had already decided on an amount. "We thought perhaps two hundred dollars. We can't go any higher than that."

It really sounded pretty good to me. "I'll take it up with Fred and Jim and get back to you as soon as I talk to them."

The more I thought about it, two hundred dollars sounded like a fair price. We had only paid fifty dollars for the old car. Of course, we bought tires and things to fix her up, but counting all the fun we had riding around in Lizzy, two hundred dollars seemed like a reasonable price. And we would be handing down a team mascot to a future generation.

When I outlined the offer to my co-owners, they quickly agreed to the deal and we each walked away sixty-six dollars richer. That was enough money to cover our prom expenses with even a little left over. We were also left with happy memories of Lizzy and the knowledge that she would continue as a fixture in Redbank for many years to come.

The junior/senior prom was a great success. The junior class had decorated the gym in red and white. Even the centerpiece on each table was an arrangement of red and white carnations. They had hired the best band in the area and their lead singer, a young lady named Janie Jamison, was really sensational. When the dance ended at eleven-thirty, Janie sang the closing song, "Goodnight Sweetheart" and all the girls cried.

Following the end of the prom, the seniors went to a special gathering at Fred Smith's house where his mother served cake and of course all flavors of ice cream. Don't forget, Fred's dad ran the local dairy. The party broke up about two o'clock in the morning and both Barb and I were really tired. Such late nights weren't the norm in Redbank.

As I lay in bed that night, I couldn't help but think of my two friends that weren't there to celebrate with us, Jack Algood and Anne Adams. What a tragic turn of events their lives had taken. I would have never guessed that Jack would meet such an untimely death in a far away place like Japan. And it seemed impossible that Anne had ended up as a bar girl in Baltimore. The path of life can certainly lead in many different directions.

Graduation Day was almost anti-climatic after such a great prom. A funny thing happened at graduation as the Superintendent of Schools was reading off the names of those being called to the platform. When he read off "John Charles White," I just sat there, not being used to hearing my full name. When no one moved, he finally said, "Will someone please wake up Jack White and tell him his given name?" The gym erupted in laughter.

EPILOGUE

SINCE THEN ...

I left for the Army as scheduled on June the third. Dad and Mom dropped me off at the recruiting station in Staunton that morning amid a stream of tears from my mother. Dad's goodbye was only a firm handshake and a hug, but I thought I could see his eyes watering up.

From Staunton things proceeded just as the recruiter had informed us they would. About twenty recruits from the area were on the bus to Arlington where we all raised our hands and swore to defend our nation against all enemies. From there it was just a short bus ride to Fort Meade, Maryland for processing.

We had a busy three days as we rushed from place to place getting our medical exams, uniforms and haircuts, as well as filling out the numerous forms that were required. Finally we boarded a train going west toward Kentucky. I was just eighteen years old and an army private.

Our basic training with the 101st Airborne Division at Camp Breckenridge lasted only eight weeks, just like we had been promised. I was then given orders to proceed to Fort Devens near Ayer,

Massachusetts for eight additional weeks of specialized training. That was my introduction to the world of military intelligence.

Apparently my instructors were pleased with how well I did in my specialized training because I graduated at the top of my class and was then sent on to a second school at the same base for another sixteen weeks. Once again I finished at the head of the class. My brain was spinning with all the new insight I had gained and I was anxious to put it into practice.

Most of my classmates received orders for Korea, but mine required me to proceed to Japan where I was attached to a civilian group of "spooks" as we were often called. The others in my office were always going off on special missions while I stayed behind a desk for the remainder of my assignment just writing reports. It certainly wasn't the exciting adventure I had anticipated when I enlisted.

When my tour in Japan was completed, I was sent back to a group known as the Defense Intelligence Agency at Arlington Hall Station located in Virginia, just across the river from Washington. When I reenlisted, I was posted to various assignments around the world for the next several years. Although I was technically in the Army, I was assigned to civilian units and wore civilian clothes. Without even putting on a uniform, I was promoted from private to corporal and ultimately to sergeant first class. My postings took me to Europe, Asia, South America and even to Africa.

About the middle of 1967 when I finally returned to the United States, I was shocked to learn that my mother had died of cancer while I was in Thailand. No one had contacted me about her sickness and death because I was "out of touch" and couldn't be reached. Following her death, my father left his insurance business, sold the house and moved to Arizona. Heartbroken over the news, I took leave and paid him a short visit. Dad and I shed a lot of tears together and I left feeling that I had really let my parents down as a son. It was hard for my dad to understand what was being demanded of me by my country.

Arriving back in Arlington, I was called into the division chief's office and asked to convert to civilian status. It seemed as though the Agency could use me better as a civilian and they were willing to offer me a much higher salary. I was informed that initially I would be assigned to a covert group in South Africa.

Knowing my strong religious convictions, it had been arranged for me to go undercover with them as a missionary working with orphanages in various African countries. Feeling that the Lord had opened the door, I gladly accepted the assignment and started working with the group. I ended up spending almost all of the next eleven years in Africa. During my time there, I was drawn more and more towards missions' work and away from the intelligence game.

It was about this time that I met a beautiful young missionary named Nancy Anderson from West Virginia. She had initially come to Africa with the Peace Corps, but soon realized that she was called more to the millions of needy orphans than the type of work that the corps was doing. When Nancy's tour with the Peace Corps was completed, she stayed on in South Africa as a full-time missionary.

The two of us were attracted to one another right from the start. In many ways she reminded me a lot of my childhood flame, Barb. Nancy loved the Lord with a great passion and we would spend countless hours studying the Bible together. Would you believe that I was still carrying the Bible that had been given to me by Max MacCormick while I was in jail? It was dog-eared and underlined with very thin pages, but I still had a deep attachment to it.

In December of 1974, I asked Nancy to marry me. She told me that she loved me but that she would never marry me as long as I was still doing undercover work for the government. On that basis, I resigned from my job with the United States government and took my retirement in South Africa.

After Nancy and I were married, I accepted a permanent job with her mission group. I refused to receive any salary from the organization because I had an excellent income from my government retirement. Together Nancy and I now oversee sixteen orphanages throughout East Africa and minister the gospel to young and old alike.

What happened to my high school friends? I kept in contact with some of them for several years.

Barbara graduated from the University of Kentucky where she was a cheerleader and a campus leader. The week after her graduation, she married an exceptional basketball player and they moved to California where he accepted a pro-basketball offer. Unfortunately it didn't work out for him, but Barb and her husband remained on the west coast where he returned to university and got his law degree. I understand that they had a couple of children, but then I lost touch.

Anne Adams was cleared of any charges and eventually inherited what was left of her father's estate. She moved out of state and no one seemed to know where she went.

Fred Smith took over the dairy and ice cream business that his dad had started and still lives in Redbank. He and his wife had five boys during their first twelve years of marriage. Fred always was a glutton for punishment.

Betty Mason followed in her father's footsteps and got her degree in education. She taught for many years in the schools of Shawnee County. I am not sure if Betty ever got married.

Redbank High School faded into oblivion when a new high school was built which consolidated both of the county's high schools into one. When that happened, it meant the end of the famed Red Raiders. Only the memories remained.

As I understand, our old car, Lizzy was a fixture around town for a couple of years, but eventually met her demise when a cattle truck rammed her head on while she was parked on a street in town.

My four high school years were a mixture of good times and bad times. *"It was the best of times, it was the worst of times."* But those years were special. They marked the years when a boy became a man.

35235837R00078

Made in the USA
Charleston, SC
02 November 2014